FROM THE
NANCY DREW FILES

THE CASE: Nancy follows a trail of dirty money, hoping to prove the innocence of a young accountant.

CONTACT: Matt Goldin is locked in prison, and it's up to Nancy to find the key that will set him free.

SUSPECTS: Peter Sands—*Matt's junior partner, he provided crucial evidence at the trial. Now he's taken control of the accounting firm.*

Johnny Spector—*he owns Over the Rainbow, a comedy club where the real funny business is in the way money comes . . . and goes.*

Bianca Engel *and* Tony Fry—*the club's assistant manager and bartender are full of schemes . . . and clearly afraid that their secret will come out.*

COMPLICATIONS: Nancy is determined to clear the name of a man whom a judge and jury have already found guilty—and Matt Goldin's own sister is doing all she can to protect a prime suspect!

Books in The Nancy Drew Files® Series

#1 SECRETS CAN KILL
#2 DEADLY INTENT
#3 MURDER ON ICE
#4 SMILE AND SAY MURDER
#5 HIT AND RUN HOLIDAY
#6 WHITE WATER TERROR
#7 DEADLY DOUBLES
#8 TWO POINTS TO MURDER
#9 FALSE MOVES
#10 BURIED SECRETS
#11 HEART OF DANGER
#12 FATAL RANSOM
#13 WINGS OF FEAR
#14 THIS SIDE OF EVIL
#15 TRIAL BY FIRE
#16 NEVER SAY DIE
#17 STAY TUNED FOR DANGER
#18 CIRCLE OF EVIL
#19 SISTERS IN CRIME
#20 VERY DEADLY YOURS
#21 RECIPE FOR MURDER
#22 FATAL ATTRACTION
#23 SINISTER PARADISE
#24 TILL DEATH DO US PART
#25 RICH AND DANGEROUS
#26 PLAYING WITH FIRE
#27 MOST LIKELY TO DIE
#28 THE BLACK WIDOW
#29 PURE POISON
#30 DEATH BY DESIGN
#31 TROUBLE IN TAHITI
#32 HIGH MARKS FOR MALICE
#33 DANGER IN DISGUISE
#34 VANISHING ACT
#35 BAD MEDICINE
#36 OVER THE EDGE
#37 LAST DANCE
#38 THE FINAL SCENE
#39 THE SUSPECT NEXT DOOR

#40 SHADOW OF A DOUBT
#41 SOMETHING TO HIDE
#42 THE WRONG CHEMISTRY
#43 FALSE IMPRESSIONS
#44 SCENT OF DANGER
#45 OUT OF BOUNDS
#46 WIN, PLACE OR DIE
#47 FLIRTING WITH DANGER
#48 A DATE WITH DECEPTION
#49 PORTRAIT IN CRIME
#50 DEEP SECRETS
#51 A MODEL CRIME
#52 DANGER FOR HIRE
#53 TRAIL OF LIES
#54 COLD AS ICE
#55 DON'T LOOK TWICE
#56 MAKE NO MISTAKE
#57 INTO THIN AIR
#58 HOT PURSUIT
#59 HIGH RISK
#60 POISON PEN
#61 SWEET REVENGE
#62 EASY MARKS
#63 MIXED SIGNALS
#64 THE WRONG TRACK
#65 FINAL NOTES
#66 TALL, DARK AND DEADLY
#67 NOBODY'S BUSINESS
#68 CROSSCURRENTS
#69 RUNNING SCARED
#70 CUTTING EDGE
#71 HOT TRACKS
#72 SWISS SECRETS
#73 RENDEZVOUS IN ROME
#74 GREEK ODYSSEY
#75 A TALENT FOR MURDER
#76 THE PERFECT PLOT
#77 DANGER ON PARADE
#78 UPDATE ON CRIME
#79 NO LAUGHING MATTER

Available from ARCHWAY Paperbacks

The Nancy Drew Files

Case 79

No Laughing Matter

Carolyn Keene

AN ARCHWAY PAPERBACK
Published by POCKET BOOKS
New York   London   Toronto   Sydney   Tokyo   Singapore

AN ARCHWAY PAPERBACK *Original*

An Archway Paperback published by
POCKET BOOKS, a division of Simon & Schuster Inc.
1230 Avenue of the Americas, New York, NY 10020

Copyright © 1993 by Simon & Schuster Inc.
Produced by Mega-Books of New York, Inc.

ISBN: 0-671-73083-5

First Archway Paperback printing January 1993

10 9 8 7 6 5 4 3 2 1

NANCY DREW, AN ARCHWAY PAPERBACK and colophon are registered trademarks of Simon & Schuster Inc.

THE NANCY DREW FILES is a trademark of Simon & Schuster Inc.

Cover art by Tricia Zimic

Printed in the U.S.A.

IL 6+

Chapter

One

"I GIVE UP on these chopsticks," Bess Marvin said, frustrated and shaking her blond hair. "At this rate I'll finish dinner by lunchtime tomorrow. Anybody else want to use a fork?"

Nancy Drew smiled at her friend from her position on the living-room carpet. "No thanks. Ned might want one," she said, ruffling her boyfriend's thick, chestnut hair. "He's been trying to get that peapod in his mouth for twenty minutes."

The three friends were sitting cross-legged around the Drews' coffee table, white paper boxes of Chinese food in front of them. A blaze in the fireplace threw a warm glow over their faces.

"I never learned how to use these things either," Ned said, throwing down his chopsticks. "I'm with you, Bess."

While Bess went into the kitchen for forks, Nancy reached over and gave Ned a warm hug. It was great to have him home from college for winter break. She'd been looking forward to it for weeks. Her detective work had been keeping her busy, and her last case, an undercover assignment in a TV newsroom, had been especially hair-raising. She hoped they'd be able to spend all their free time together during Ned's break.

"What's that for?" Ned asked softly as he pulled back from the hug.

"Actually, it's a message from George," Nancy said, grinning at him. "She's in Utah, skiing with her parents, but she told me to give you a hug for her. So consider yourself hugged."

Bess returned from the kitchen with two forks and handed one to Ned. "What do you have planned for vacation?" she asked him.

"A little work. A little play. Oh, and a trip to prison," Ned replied.

"Planning to get caught committing a major crime, Nickerson?" Nancy joked, raising an eyebrow. She scooped up the last bite of food with her chopsticks and popped it into her mouth.

Ned shook his head as he finished swallowing a forkful of spicy chicken and cashew nuts. "The trip's for my business ethics class. We're going to talk to a few inmates at a minimum-security prison tomorrow," he explained. "Our teacher wants us to learn how and why people commit white-collar crimes—"

"Wait a second," Bess interrupted, holding up a hand. "I always hear that expression, but I'm not really sure what it means."

"Well, white-collar crimes are the kind you can commit while working in administrative jobs," Ned explained. "Say you worked in a bank and used the computer system to steal money from people's accounts. That would be a white-collar crime."

Nancy reached for a paper napkin from the pile on the coffee table. "White-collar crimes usually aren't violent, like murder or armed robbery," she added. "They're mostly crimes that are committed on paper."

"Still, they sound serious," Bess put in.

Ned agreed. Putting down his fork, he leaned against the sofa and stretched his long legs out in front of him. "That's precisely why my professor wants us to talk to white-collar criminals about how they got involved in their crimes."

"It would be a good way to scare students into staying clean," Nancy commented. "Which prison are you going to visit?"

"It's called Fairwood. You know, the one just outside River Heights."

"The one Matt Goldin was sent to," Bess said, finishing up the last of her rice.

Ned raised an eyebrow. "Who's he?"

"I don't know if you ever met Lisa Goldin. She

3

went to high school with us," Nancy said. "Her brother, Matt, was the accountant for the comedy club Over the Rainbow. He got caught stealing money from them a few months back."

Bess shook her head. "It's still hard to believe. I don't know Matt that well, but he didn't seem like the kind of guy who'd do something illegal." Getting to her feet, she asked, "Are you guys done eating?"

Nancy nodded, and she and Ned helped Bess stack dishes and collect the food containers. While they loaded the dishwasher, Nancy kept thinking about Ned's project. She'd always been fascinated by what made criminals break the law. . . .

"The answer is yes, Nan," Ned said out of the blue.

Nancy shot her boyfriend a puzzled glance. He was smiling at her, his brown eyes shining mischievously. "I knew you'd be intrigued by my visit to Fairwood, so I asked Professor Greer if you could come," Ned explained. "She said it'd be fine."

"I'd love to go. Thanks," Nancy said, kissing him on the cheek.

"Just make sure they know you're there only for a visit, Nancy," Bess said with a giggle. She wiped her hands on a towel and sat down at the kitchen table. "Now, the moment we've all been waiting for—time to open the fortune cookies."

She tore open the plastic bag containing the three cookies and handed it around.

Ned read his fortune first. " 'No matter how much bleach, white collar still gets dirty,' " he said.

Bess's mouth dropped open. "That's so weird!" she exclaimed, glancing from Nancy to Ned.

Nancy had noticed that Ned was having a hard time keeping a straight face. "Um, Bess, I think he's joking," she said.

"I can't believe I fell for that!" Bess said, punching Ned's arm. "What does it really say?"

Ned smiled at Nancy. "A visit to your girlfriend will make you very happy."

At nine-thirty Monday morning, Nancy pulled into Ned's driveway and honked her horn. Almost instantly Ned bounded out the front door, pulling on his ski jacket while balancing a piece of toast, his gloves, and a notebook. Nancy couldn't believe how cute he looked.

"Hi!" he said, greeting her. "Thanks for picking me up. My car will be out of the shop today, so you won't have to ferry me around anymore."

Nancy tapped the tip of his nose. "No problem. We get to spend a little more time together."

The drive back toward River Heights from Mapleton, where Ned lived, went quickly. A few miles past River Heights Nancy spotted a small sign at the side of the highway that read "Fairwood Correctional Facility." She turned off and made her way up a long drive that curved through a stand of trees.

Ned squinted through the windshield as they rounded a sharp curve. "This place doesn't look much like a prison," he commented.

Nancy took in the group of low brown buildings beyond the trees. The buildings were all joined by enclosed walkways. They were very ordinary, except for the metal grates over the windows. "It's a minimum-security facility, so I guess that explains why there's no barbed wire above the gates or towers with guards."

A few moments later Nancy pulled her Mustang into a space in the crowded visitors' parking lot. The cold morning air made her pull her parka tight around herself as they followed the signs to the visitors' entrance.

Inside, fluorescent light brightened the garish yellow walls to almost blinding. Nancy and Ned stopped at the visitors' check-in counter. A tall man with receding dark hair and deep creases etched into his forehead sat behind the counter. His name tag read Sam Jenkins, Assistant Warden.

"May I help you?" he asked in a gravelly voice.

When Ned explained why they were there, the assistant warden had them sign the visitors' register. "Ms. Greer's group is assembled in the lecture room. I'll show you down there."

He poked his head through a doorway behind the counter and said, "Cover for me, will you, Petra?"

The assistant warden then led Nancy and Ned down a hall into a larger building. Their footsteps echoed off the walls as they passed one open doorway after another. Mr. Jenkins pointed out the prisoners' computer room, library, and one of the guard booths.

"I guess you're not too worried about security," Ned commented as an inmate, dressed in khaki pants and a blue shirt, walked by all alone.

"This is more a work camp than a prison," Mr. Jenkins responded. "The other side of this building is the main cell area. The men live four to a room with a door that closes to give them some privacy. They have work schedules, but they get to choose what to do when. That's the toughest part for a lot of these guys.

"When you're on the outside, all you want is free time. In here, too much free time makes you crazy. These guys want to know what they're doing every minute of every day. By keeping busy, they feel the time they spend here is somehow worthwhile."

A moment later they entered what looked like a large, comfortable classroom. About a dozen of Ned's classmates were sitting in the rows of folding chairs. Five inmates were at the front of the room, talking to a robust woman with chocolate-colored skin and alert brown eyes.

7

"That's Professor Greer," Ned whispered. He started introducing Nancy to some of his classmates but stopped when the teacher turned to the class and spoke.

"I'm glad to see you all made it this morning," she began. "We all know why we're here, so let's get started." She gestured to a short, heavyset inmate who had thinning dark hair.

"Hi, I'm Dennis Lassiter. I'd like to welcome the Emerson students to Fairwood," the inmate said, getting to his feet. "The last time I spoke in front of a group of people they were all lying on the floor, with their hands up. Just kidding," he added quickly. A few students giggled nervously. "I'm serving time for money laundering. Anybody want to take a crack at what that means?"

A girl with fair hair and glasses raised her hand. "Making dirty money clean?"

"Exactly," Dennis Lassiter said with a smile. He seemed so charming and friendly. It was hard to believe that he could have done anything wrong.

"Dirty money is money that is made illegally," the prisoner continued. "For example, certain types of gambling are illegal in this state. I made a lot of money by gambling, so I had to make it look as if I had earned it in a legal way. What I did was pretend that I made the money in my grocery business—that my business made more money and spent more money than it really did."

Professor Greer spoke up from the edge of the room. "Can anybody guess how to do that?"

Ned raised his hand. "You'd write false receipts for things you sold and things you bought."

"That's exactly what I did. I made up sales receipts for food that I never sold, so it looked like I made more money than I really did. Then I created a phony supply company and made up bills to show that I bought a lot of groceries from them. I even opened an account for the supply company, where I deposited all the money I made from gambling. But I kept careful records of the fake receipts so that I could fool my accountant, the tax men, and the government."

Glancing around, Nancy saw amazement on the students' faces. They seemed to be as surprised as she was that this unassuming man would have tried to pull off this hoax.

Dennis Lassiter paused for a moment and took a deep breath. "You're probably all wondering why I committed this crime."

Nancy *had* been asking herself that question. Dennis Lassiter seemed so smart and sensible. Why did he have to launder money when it seemed as if he had a successful business?

"It's very simple," Lassiter said. "I was greedy, and I didn't think I'd ever get caught. Just about everybody in here will tell you the same thing."

After he had finished talking, the students

asked questions and other inmates joined in the informal discussion. They talked about other white-collar crimes: forgery, credit-card fraud, and embezzlement. Then Professor Greer thanked the inmates and informed the students that they'd be taking a tour of the prison.

"But first we've been invited to have some refreshments," Professor Greer said, gesturing toward the back of the room.

Turning in her chair, Nancy saw that a table was being set up with coffee, hot chocolate, doughnuts, and fresh fruit. Her heart leapt when she noticed the brown-haired, bearded inmate who was in charge of the food. It was Matt Goldin!

His face was more gaunt than Nancy remembered, and his blue workshirt hung loosely from his shoulders. Matt's trial had ended just a few weeks earlier, but already he'd lost a noticeable amount of weight.

"Ned, you won't believe . . ." Nancy's voice trailed off when she realized that Ned was talking to Dennis Lassiter at the front of the room. Taking a deep breath, Nancy started in Matt's direction. She didn't know what she'd say to him, but she couldn't just ignore him.

"Nancy! I thought that was you."

Matt was trying to smile, but only one side of his mouth turned up. His skin was pale, and there were circles under his brown eyes. "Can I talk to you a minute—alone?" he asked, trembling slightly.

"Uh, sure," she replied. Nancy wasn't sure whether it was okay to leave the rest of the group, but Matt seemed so upset that she couldn't say no.

She followed him out of the lecture room and into the hallway.

"Nancy, you're the only one who can help me," Matt said urgently.

"What do you mean? How can I help?" she asked. Matt had already been convicted. She didn't know what she could possibly do for him now.

Matt fixed her with a desperate gaze. "I didn't steal that money from Over the Rainbow. I was framed!"

Chapter

Two

NANCY WAS STUNNED. She wanted to believe Matt. He didn't seem like a criminal, but who would have thought that Dennis Lassiter was a crook, either?

"You've got to believe me, Nancy," Matt insisted. Under the harsh fluorescent lights, his face was ghostlike.

"Tell me what happened," Nancy said calmly, leaning against the wall to listen.

Matt took a deep breath, raking a hand through his hair. "Well, you know I had my own accounting firm, GS Accounting Associates," he began. "Over the Rainbow was one of my biggest clients. About six months ago I was going over their books and I noticed that they had suddenly started doing terrific business. They were making twice as much money as they had only a few months before."

"So you got suspicious?" Nancy guessed.

"First I tried to justify it," Matt explained. "The club had just gotten a hot new MC, Rusty Smith, and he brought in other really good comics. I thought, well, maybe business has really improved. But realistically I knew there was no way the club could be bringing in that kind of money."

Matt glanced nervously over his shoulder before continuing. "I started going through the club's receipts very carefully. I didn't recognize the names of some of the companies the club bought supplies from, and some of the receipts just had amounts listed. What the club had bought wasn't itemized."

Matt's story was beginning to sound like what Dennis Lassiter had described, Nancy realized. "You mean you thought they were laundering money?" she asked.

He nodded. "I had no proof, though. So one night I went to the club to see what kind of crowd came in and how much they ate and drank. I stayed around until the end of the evening, and then I asked Bianca Engel—she's the assistant manager—how much money they'd taken in. She acted strange and told me she'd check on it.

"The place was practically empty, so I decided to check out the main cash register to see if there were any receipts tucked away."

Nancy stared at him. "Didn't you think someone would see you?"

"It seemed like the right thing to do at the time," Matt said miserably. "I had my hands on a bunch of credit-card receipts when the bartender, Tony Fry, caught me. Of course he thought I was trying to rob them, so he started screaming, 'Get the blasted cops!' He's British and very excitable."

Nancy noticed that Matt was beginning to sweat. Telling this story was obviously upsetting him.

"It looked bad, especially since there were several hundred-dollar bills stuck to the receipts I had fished out of the cash drawer," Matt went on. "I told Tony I was just looking for a key to the office upstairs, but I wasn't very convincing."

"What did he do?" Nancy asked.

"The owner, Johnny, had come over by then. He's a pretty easygoing guy. He kind of laughed the whole thing off. But I felt as if he didn't quite trust me after that. Then this whole thing happened. . . ."

Matt's voice trailed off as Ned walked out of the lecture room. "Oh, there you are, Nan," Ned said.

Nancy introduced Ned to Matt. "You can trust Ned to be discreet, too," she told Matt.

"Listen, why don't I show you around while I tell you the rest of the story," Matt suggested.

After telling Professor Greer they'd be taking a brief tour, Nancy and Ned rejoined Matt. He led them to his room. Inside there were two sets of bunk beds, a couple of straight-back chairs, and a desk. Some effort had been made to add personal touches to the room. Nancy noticed a picture of Matt and his sister, Lisa, pinned beside a top bunk. Matt followed her gaze, then quickly looked away.

"I'll be right back," he said. "I have to inform my supervisor that I'm with you."

While he was gone, Nancy quickly filled Ned in on what Matt had already told her.

"Wow!" Ned let out a low whistle. "Do you think he was really framed?"

"I don't know," Nancy said with a shrug. "I guess it's possible, but I wonder why—"

She broke off as Matt returned. He gestured for them to sit in the two chairs, while he perched on a bottom bunk. "I keep hoping I'll wake up one morning and find out this is all a nightmare," he said, sighing deeply.

"Nancy's already told me a bit about your suspicions of money laundering at Over the Rainbow," Ned said gently.

"It's too bad I got arrested before I could prove anything," Matt said, shaking his head. "About a week after the cash register incident, I was arrested for embezzling money from Over the Rainbow. The police claimed that I had opened an account under the name Gold Enterprises.

The account had ten thousand dollars in it—a check from Over the Rainbow for that amount had been deposited. My signature was on the check and on the bank's signature card to open the account. At the trial a bank teller testified that I had opened the account, but I didn't."

This sounded like a frame-up, all right—if Matt Goldin was telling the truth. "Couldn't your lawyer prove you were innocent?" Nancy asked.

"He tried, but there wasn't enough evidence to prove I was being framed. I even hired a private investigator, a guy named Keith O'Brien."

Nancy's next question was drowned out by an amplified voice coming from the hallway: "Paging Ned Nickerson. Please join your group in the warden's office."

"I guess that's our cue to leave," Ned said apologetically, getting to his feet.

Nancy paused at the doorway. There wasn't enough time to ask all the questions swirling in her head, but she had to ask just one. "Matt, do you have any idea who framed you?"

Matt rubbed his chin thoughtfully as he got up from the bunk. "I hate to even think this, but before my arrest, Peter Sands, my junior partner, was getting more and more dissatisfied. He felt that I wasn't giving him the big accounts. The truth is, I didn't think he could handle them yet. He was the one who found the canceled check that was deposited in the Gold Enterprises account. He said that I had accidentally left the check in the file of one of his clients, but I know I didn't."

"So you think it's possible he was in on the money-laundering operation?" Ned asked. "Or that he was paid off by the people behind the operation?"

"Anybody with access to the accounting books could have been involved," Matt told him. "The owner, Johnny, barely pays any attention. He's mostly there to enjoy the comedy—kind of like a figurehead. Everybody knows him. When I tried to talk to him about taxes and receipts, he turned the conversation to the great old comedians."

Matt looked imploringly from Nancy to Ned. "Do you think you can help me?"

"I'll check into it," Nancy agreed, smiling at Matt. She wasn't sure she could really help him, but she would do her best to get at the truth.

"Matt was desperate for someone to believe him, so I said I'd check it out," Nancy told Bess over the phone early that evening. She held the phone to her ear with one hand while she applied mascara with the other, peering into the mirror over her dresser.

"I hope he really is innocent," Bess's voice came back over the line.

Just then Nancy heard a car pull into the driveway. "Ned's here," she told Bess. "I have to go. See you at the party." Cindy Ribelow, a friend of Bess's, had decided to prolong the holiday season with a post–New Year's party. When Bess invited Nancy and Ned to come along, Nancy had jumped at the chance. After her morning at Fairwood, she needed some fun.

Nancy gave a final brush to her long reddish blond hair and quickly surveyed her outfit. Her blue sweater matched her eyes, and the jeans hugged her slender figure. After giving her reflection an approving nod, she ran down the stairs, grabbed her fleece-lined leather jacket from the hall closet, and hurried to the door. She opened it to find Ned standing there, ready to knock.

"You look great," he said, bending down to give her a soft kiss that sent a pleasant shudder up and down her spine.

"You look pretty good yourself," she returned, glancing at the fisherman's sweater and corduroys he was wearing under his open parka.

After they climbed into his car, Ned said, "I need your advice, Detective Drew. I decided that Matt Goldin's case would be perfect for my business ethics paper, but I'm not sure he's telling the truth. What do you think?"

Nancy buckled her seat belt and settled back against the cracked vinyl seat while Ned backed out of her driveway. "I want to believe him, but the only way to prove he's innocent—or guilty— is to do a little investigating."

"Well, I've got a head start on you," Ned said, grinning at her. "Before I came over here, I went to Over the Rainbow and talked to Bianca Engel, the assistant manager. She wasn't helpful at all. In fact, I got the cold shoulder. She just said that they wanted to put the whole incident behind them and that if I was curious about the case I should read the newspaper accounts and talk to Matt's lawyer."

"She's right about talking to Matt's lawyer, anyway," Nancy said. "But she does sound—"

"What's this guy's problem?" Ned interrupted her, gazing up at his rearview mirror.

Nancy turned in her seat to check behind them. A van with a pair of powerful headlights was bearing down on them. "The driver's crazy to be going so fast," she said, squinting into the glare. Facing forward again, she tugged on her seat belt to make sure it was secure.

Ned pushed down on the gas pedal to put a little distance between them and the van, but the van quickly closed it. The driver probably just wanted to pass, Nancy reasoned. She saw that Ned was hunched forward in his seat, his jaw set as he concentrated on the road that was leading onto a bridge.

The van was a few feet from their rear bumper now, Nancy saw as she glanced out the rear window again. The white haze from the headlights made it impossible to see the license plate, but she could just make out that the van was white, with a stripe across the front. Its bumper seemed to be twisted and bent.

"Ned, maybe you should slow down," Nancy suggested.

Before Ned could answer, the van rammed them. Nancy's heart jumped into her throat as the jolt threw her back against the seat.

"I'm out of control!" Ned cried as his car skidded and swerved wildly.

Nancy gasped when she looked out the front windshield. In a moment they were going to crash into the guardrail and plunge into the river below.

Chapter

Three

Nancy held her arms straight in front of her, bracing them against the dashboard, her heart pounding like crazy. She heard her own voice talking, but it seemed as if it was coming from someone else. "Easy, Ned. You've got it."

Ned turned the steering wheel hard to the left, away from the edge of the bridge. A little loose gravel flew out from the screeching wheels, but the tires finally caught and the car swung left. As Ned brought the car to a full stop, the van whizzed past.

Nancy felt as if an eternity had elapsed in the past few seconds. All she could do was sit still, gulping in air.

"Are you okay, Nan?" Ned asked, his voice husky. He reached over to touch her shoulder, and Nancy could feel his hand shaking.

"I-I'm okay," she replied. "That was some fancy driving, Nickerson." They both giggled from nervous tension. "I couldn't get a plate number," Nancy went on, "but it was a white compact van, with a twisted front bumper. It had a stripe across the front. Blue, I think."

Ned looked at her appreciatively. "Only Nancy Drew would notice all that in the middle of being run off a bridge." He steered the car across the bridge and pulled up on the shoulder on the far side. "Come here," he said, unbuckling her seat belt. She scooted closer so he could put an arm around her.

"Ned, who do you think that was?" Nancy spoke into the collar of his parka, then pulled back to take in her boyfriend's face. "Could someone from Over the Rainbow have followed you? Did you notice anyone behind you before you got to my house?"

Ned frowned for a moment, thinking. "Wait a second," he said, slapping the steering wheel. "I do remember seeing a white compact van parked in the lot. I only noticed it because it was taking up two spaces. I didn't really pay any attention after I left, though. If the van followed me, I didn't notice."

"Well, if it *was* the same van, my guess is that someone didn't like your asking questions at Over the Rainbow. And whoever it was was worried enough to scare you. It's probably a message for you to stop asking questions."

"Which makes me think there might be some truth to Matt's story," Ned added.

Nancy drummed her fingers on the dashboard. "Was the assistant manager the only person you talked to? Did anyone else hear?"

"The bartender was hanging around," Ned told her. "And a guy with red hair was talking with an older man in a suit. I think the older guy was the owner."

Nancy shot her boyfriend a worried glance. "Well, someone there has made you a target. This project could turn out to be dangerous, Ned."

"Hey, I can handle it," he said, pulling out onto the road. "But for right now, I'm in the mood to party!"

Cindy Ribelow's party was in full swing by the time Nancy and Ned arrived. Through the front window they saw a crowd dancing in the living room, while smaller groups hung out, talking and eating.

"Hi, Nancy!" Cindy said when she answered the door. Nancy had met the energetic blond-haired girl a few times at Bess's house. "And you must be Ned, right?"

"Guilty," Ned told Cindy, grinning. He and Nancy squeezed their jackets into an already stuffed closet, then surveyed the living room while Cindy excused herself to open the door again.

"Nancy! Ned!" Bess called, waving from

across the room. Her bright red jumpsuit stood out in the crowd, and it set off her petite, curvy figure.

"I'll catch up with you in a minute," Ned said, eyeing salads, salsa and chips, and desserts on the dining-room table, just beyond an arched doorway.

"Try not to inhale everything at once," Nancy said, grinning at her boyfriend.

As she made her way across the crowded living room, Nancy saw that Bess was talking to Lisa Goldin, a petite girl with olive skin and sad brown eyes.

"It's such a mess!" Lisa was saying as Nancy walked up to her and Bess. "I'm sure that Matt didn't do it, but it's so hard to prove."

Turning to Nancy, Lisa added, "Bess told me that you saw my brother at Fairwood today. I hope you can help prove that he was set up."

"I'm certainly going to check into what's going on at Over the Rainbow," Nancy promised. "I want to talk to Matt's lawyer, too. Do you know his name?"

Lisa frowned, groping for the name. "Irwin? Yeah, that's it. Tom Irwin. He's with a firm called Martel and Donnelson."

Nancy wasn't sure how to phrase her next question, so she just asked it point-blank. "Lisa, do you think your brother is innocent?"

"I *know* that Matt didn't steal that money!" Lisa said adamantly.

"What about his junior partner, Peter Sands?" Nancy asked. "When I talked to Matt, he said that Peter may have had something to do with framing him."

Panic flashed into Lisa's brown eyes. "Peter's just not that kind of person," she said, focusing first on Bess, then on Nancy. "Matt shouldn't be spreading rumors about him."

Nancy was surprised at Lisa's reaction. Why was she defending Peter so strongly against her own brother?

"Peter's working night and day," Lisa went on coolly. Her attitude toward Nancy had visibly stiffened. "Since Matt went on trial, business has really gone downhill. Peter's fighting to hold things together."

She rubbed her temples wearily, then said, "I have a really bad headache. I'm going to say goodbye to Cindy and go home."

As Lisa made her way back toward the foyer, Bess grimaced at Nancy. "I guess we hit a sore spot," Bess said. "She definitely didn't like what Matt said about Peter."

"Mmm. I wonder why—especially since Peter Sands helped put her brother in jail," Nancy said, more to herself than to Bess.

Nancy was quiet as she tried to think of where to start her investigation. Matt had been arrested six months earlier. If he *had* been set up, it wouldn't be easy to find evidence. The person who had framed him had had six months to cover his or her tracks. Still, Nancy could contact Peter Sands, Matt's lawyer, and—

She snapped her fingers as an idea came to her. "The only way I'm going to get closer to the truth is to get inside Over the Rainbow," she told Bess. "Do they serve food and drinks there?"

"Sure," Bess replied. "They have a great menu. People eat and drink while the comedians are on stage."

"Do you think they'd hire me as a waitress?"

"In a flash," Bess answered. "I'm sure they need extra help. Over the Rainbow has gotten really popular since they hired a new comic from Chicago, Rusty Smith. He's hysterical!"

"You've seen his show?"

Bess nodded. "A couple of times. And I saw him once on one of those comedy channels on cable. He happens to be totally gorgeous as well as funny."

"Bess, get a grip," Nancy said, laughing. "Listen, do you think it's too late to go over there now to see if I can get a job? I hate to leave the party, but I want to start investigating as soon as possible. Matt's future could depend on it."

Bess nodded across the room to where Ned was talking to a blond-haired guy. They were both devouring brownies. "Do you think we can tear Ned away from the food?"

"Actually, I don't think he should go with us," Nancy said. She briefly told Bess about the white van that had rammed them.

"Nancy, that's awful!" Bess exclaimed, her blue eyes wide. "You guys could have been seriously hurt!"

"It was pretty scary," Nancy agreed. "That's why I don't want anyone from the club to see him. If they realize that we know Ned, we could all be in danger."

"Here we are," Bess announced, pulling her red Camaro into the parking lot of a small complex of buildings.

The complex was in an area that had been run-down until a developer renovated it recently. Now it was a bustling commercial district that was especially popular with teenagers. There was a dance club, a pizzeria, and Over the Rainbow.

As she and Bess got out in the parking lot, Nancy checked for the white van but didn't see it anywhere. The girls' breath made white puffs in the cold air as they hurried to the entrance, which was lit up by a stylized neon sign. When they opened the door, they found themselves in a spacious, rectangular room with exposed brick walls and a stage at one end. Round café tables took up most of the floor space near the stage. At the opposite end of the club were the bar, an old-fashioned jukebox, and double doors leading to the kitchen.

"Looks like the last show is over," Nancy said, glancing at the empty stage. People were getting up from their tables, paying their checks, and leaving.

"I wonder who we should talk to about getting a job," Bess said in a low voice. "Do you think that manager Ned talked to is here now?"

As Nancy glanced around the club, her attention was caught by a man and woman behind the beverage counter. The man was tall, with very pale skin, dark hair, and hazel eyes. He was dressed in black jeans and a white button-down shirt, and he was talking urgently to a petite, slender woman with a headful of auburn curls. They were both in their early twenties.

"So, what did you tell him?" the man asked in a heavy British accent.

Probably Tony, Nancy decided. The bartender who had caught Matt with his hands in the cash register. Turning to Bess, Nancy put a finger to her lips and took a step closer to the bar. She deliberately turned her back to the man and woman so they wouldn't suspect that she was listening, but all of her attention was focused on what they were saying.

"He was asking a lot of questions about what we were doing and when," the woman replied. "I didn't answer anything directly."

"Well, we took care of him. He won't be nosing around asking questions anymore," the guy said.

Nancy's eyes widened. It sounded as if they

were talking about Ned! She had to hold herself back from whirling around and confronting the guy, but she knew she couldn't give herself away.

"We can't have this leak out," the woman said. "If Johnny ever finds out, we're dead."

Chapter

Four

Nᴀɴᴄʏ'ѕ ᴍɪɴᴅ was whirling. If they were talking about Ned, that could mean that these two had a hand in framing Matt and that there really was a money-laundering operation—or *something* illegal—going on.

"May I help you girls?"

The woman's voice broke into Nancy's thoughts. As she turned around, Nancy saw that the man and woman were staring at her and Bess.

"Um, hi!" Nancy said. She introduced herself and Bess, then said, "I wanted to speak to the manager about getting a job."

The woman's face relaxed into a smile. "I'm Bianca Engel, the assistant manager," she said, sweeping auburn curls from her eyes. "And this is Tony Fry, our bartender. As a matter of fact, we are a little short-handed right now. Do you have any waitressing experience?"

"I've worked in a few different restaurants," Nancy explained. She didn't add that it had been when she was working on cases!

"Well, I'll know soon enough, firsthand, if you know what you're doing," Bianca said. "I won't bother with checking your references. We open at five and have two shows—one at seven and one at nine. The restaurant starts serving at five-thirty. Come in at four tomorrow afternoon, and I'll show you the specifics of this restaurant."

Tony leaned over the counter and extended his hand to Nancy. "Let me be the first to welcome you formally into our humble family of over-worked and underpaid workers. Consider me your partner in crime."

Nancy chuckled nervously. She didn't miss the glare that Bianca shot at Tony. If the two *were* involved in something illegal, Bianca didn't want Tony advertising that fact—even jokingly.

"We've got to close up now," Bianca said. She lifted a hinged panel in the counter and stepped out from behind the bar. "See you tomorrow, Nancy. Nice meeting you."

Nancy barely got the word *thanks* out of her mouth before Bianca headed for a staircase at the back of the club.

"Ladies," Tony said, lifting an imaginary hat from his head and bowing slightly. Then he busied himself at the far end of the counter.

The moment he had stepped out of earshot, Bess let out a breath. "Did you hear what they said?" she asked in a whisper. "It sounds like they're the ones who ran you and Ned off the road!"

"I thought the same thing," Nancy said. "They must be involved in something illegal if they'd do something that extreme to keep Ned from sticking his nose in their business."

Bess giggled. "You mean in their dirty laundry."

Both girls pivoted around together as a man with flaming red hair stormed out onto the stage. He was followed by a young woman.

"Sandra, I can't believe you're picking this moment to fly to London to do a play. We're in the middle of a run here," the man said, throwing up his hands.

"Rusty, stop being so dramatic," the young woman said patiently. "It's a great play and a fantastic opportunity for me. I know you'll be able to find someone else for this sketch."

"What a nightmare," Rusty said. Hopping off the stage, he threw himself into a chair at one of the nearby tables and let his head fall into his hands.

After a long moment he raised his head and smiled at the woman. "The last thing I'd do is get between you and fame. Think of me when you're dripping with diamonds and furs and the queen knights you—"

"Oh, Rusty," Sandra said, giggling as she sat down next to him. "I wish I could take you with me."

"No, I'm happy right here on the stage of Over the Rainbow. Of course, I'd be happier if I had a new partner for our sketch."

Rusty stood up, put one leg on his chair, and struck a dramatic pose. "Well, I'm off, Mrs. Cleaver."

Suddenly Bess piped up: "Mr. Cleaver, you won't be needing that ax today, I suppose."

Nancy, Rusty, and Sandra all stared at Bess in surprise. Then Rusty resumed his pose and answered Bess in character: "Now, come on, Lizzy. I'm a lumberjack. How am I supposed to go to work without my ax?"

Bess and Rusty continued the silly conversation, which Nancy finally realized must be part of one of Rusty's sketches. When the sketch was finished, Rusty and Sandra both clapped and hooted. Bess turned bright red as the other two came over to join her and Nancy.

"Where did you learn that?" Rusty asked.

"I've watched it a few times here at the club," Bess told him. "I think it's hilarious. I'm Bess Marvin, by the way, and this is Nancy Drew."

Rusty introduced himself and Sandra, then asked, "How would you like to fill in for Sandra for a few days, until I find a replacement?"

Bess's mouth fell open. "Are you kidding?"

Her blue eyes opened wide as Nancy gave her the thumbs up. "I'd love to!" Bess told Rusty.

"Well, then, you're officially hired," Rusty said. "Meet me here tomorrow afternoon at one, and we'll rehearse."

"I'll be here," Bess said. Saying goodnight, she and Nancy left the club.

"Can you believe our luck?" Bess was practically jumping up and down. "Now we'll both be undercover!"

Nancy nodded. "You can try to find out if Rusty or the other comedians know anything about money laundering here at the club, or about Matt's frame-up. I'll concentrate on checking out Tony, Bianca, and the other club staff."

The night had turned icy cold. As they headed for Bess's Camaro, Nancy heard the throbbing bass of dance music from the club next door. A well-dressed couple in their forties had just gotten out of a sleek sedan next to Bess's car, and they crossed the lot toward Caribou, the dance club.

"That's odd," Nancy commented. "They look kind of old to be going to a club where they play loud rock."

"Maybe they're young at heart," Bess said, shrugging. "Actually, I've been meaning to check out Caribou myself. Maybe we can go there after work some night."

Nancy nodded vaguely. She loved to dance but

didn't think she'd really enjoy herself until she'd solved her case.

"Dad, if Matt is telling the truth, then I have to find out who framed him," Nancy said the next morning. She leaned across the dining-room table to pour her father a fresh cup of coffee, then filled her own cup.

As a prominent criminal lawyer, Carson Drew often gave Nancy valuable legal advice on her cases. Nancy had been glad to catch him before he left for his office so she could fill him in on the Matt Goldin case.

Pushing aside the morning paper, Carson gave Nancy his full attention. "From what you say, those two people at the comedy club sound like a good place to start investigating," he said.

"It might be hard for me to get any proof, though," Nancy said. "After all, Matt was arrested six months ago. My only hope is that someone was sloppy and didn't do a good job. Or that I'll be able to find evidence of the money-laundering operation."

Carson settled back in his chair. "It sounds tough. Even if there *was* money laundering going on, it may have stopped after Matt started asking questions. Do you have any leads other than Bianca and Tony?"

Nancy quickly filled her father in on Matt's suspicions of his partner, Peter Sands. "I'm going to talk to Matt's lawyer and to the PI he hired, to see what I can find out about Sands and about any money laundering at Over the Rainbow."

"I've got a trial to prepare for, but keep me posted," her father said. After getting up from the table, he kissed her cheek, grabbed his briefcase from the floor, and headed for the front hall. "Call me if you need anything."

"Thanks, Dad. See you later."

Nancy went into the kitchen and opened the River Heights phone book for the phone numbers for Martel and Donnelson, Matt's lawyer's law firm, and for Keith O'Brien, the private detective Matt had hired.

It might not be easy to come up with leads in the case, Nancy thought, but she was going to give it her best shot!

It was late morning when Nancy arrived at the offices of Martel and Donnelson. After giving her name to the receptionist, Nancy sat on a plush velour couch in the waiting area and flipped through a magazine.

"Hi, you must be Nancy Drew. I'm Tom Irwin."

Nancy raised her eyes to see a young blond-haired man in his late twenties smiling down at her. His suit was rumpled, and there were dark circles under his eyes, as if he hadn't been getting much sleep. "Are you related to Carson Drew?" he asked, holding out his hand.

"He's my father," Nancy replied, getting to her feet and shaking his hand. She followed him to his office and stepped inside. Papers and books were stacked on the desk, shelves, and even on the chair that Mr. Irwin offered her. She had never seen so much disorganization in one room.

"You'll have to excuse the mess, but I've got a trial coming up in two days and I'm a little behind schedule," the lawyer said apologetically, sweeping the books from Nancy's chair before she sat down. "Now, what was it you wanted to see me about?"

"Matt Goldin," she reminded him, trying to stifle her annoyance. She had told him what she wanted when she'd called to set up the appointment. "Matt thinks he was set up, and I'd like to know if you came up with any evidence during the trial to back up his claim."

"Matt Goldin, Matt Goldin," muttered Mr. Irwin. "Nice guy, beard, right?"

Nancy nodded, surprised that a lawyer would have forgotten a client so quickly. After all, the trial had ended only a month before.

"It's a trial I'd like to forget, since we lost. Now, where did I put his file?" Mr. Irwin said as if reading Nancy's thoughts. "Ah—here we go," he said, pulling a folder out of a stack and opening it.

Nancy waited while he skimmed the contents of the file. Finally he looked up at her again.

"That's right, the embezzling case. Matt was

sure he was set up, that there was money laundering going on at Over the Rainbow," he said. "But you know, I didn't find any evidence of it. I checked the club's books, receipts—everything. They all seemed to be in order."

"Do *you* think it's possible he was being set up?" Nancy asked.

Tom Irwin rubbed his chin and glanced down at the contents of the folder again. "I guess you already know about the account that was opened in the name of Gold Enterprises," he said. When Nancy nodded, he added, "A teller at the North Central Bank testified that Matt Goldin had opened that account. Even though Matt told me he'd never been in the bank, the teller picked him out in the courtroom."

"Was his signature checked?"

"Yes," Irwin replied. "We brought in two handwriting analysts. One was sure it was Matt's signature. The other was less sure but, in the end, decided that it was Matt's, too."

So far Tom hadn't provided her with any new leads, Nancy reflected. In fact, he seemed so disorganized and overworked that she wouldn't be surprised if he had overlooked some important clue during the trial. "What about Peter Sands, Matt's partner?" she probed. "He's the one who found the check, right?"

Mr. Irwin nodded. "What struck me was that Sands didn't go to Matt with the check before contacting the police," he said. "But when I asked Sands about it on the stand, he said that their partnership had deteriorated to the point where he didn't trust Matt."

The junior accountant's explanation seemed a little weak to Nancy, but Tom Irwin couldn't offer her any more information. I guess I'll just have to find out more about Peter Sands myself, she reflected.

After getting the name and telephone number of the bank teller, and the address of Matt's accounting firm, Nancy thanked the lawyer and left his office. She was just stepping through the law firm's heavy outer door when the receptionist called out to her.

"Miss Drew, you've got a phone call."

That's weird, Nancy thought to herself. She didn't think anyone knew she was there.

The receptionist led her into an empty office, handed Nancy the telephone receiver, then pressed the button on the blinking line.

"Hello? This is Nancy Drew," Nancy said into the receiver.

"People shouldn't stick their noses where they don't belong," a muffled whisper came over the line.

Nancy's whole body tensed. "Who is this?" she demanded.

"Never mind that," the voice said. "Just watch your back, Miss Drew."

Then the line went dead.

Chapter

Five

Nancy slowly replaced the phone in its cradle. Someone was trying to scare her off the case. But who?

"Is everything all right?"

The receptionist was hovering in the doorway, a concerned expression on her face.

"Yes, everything's fine," Nancy fibbed. "Thanks for your help." Hurrying past the woman, she left the office.

She made her way back to her Mustang, deep in thought. How could anyone have known she'd be at the lawyer's office? She had only just made the appointment that morning. The voice had been muffled, and she didn't know if it was a man or a woman. Could Bianca and Tony have become suspicious of Nancy after she'd overheard their conversation the night before? If so, they might have followed her, then made the call.

Nancy shivered at the thought. As she emerged from the office building, she checked carefully but didn't spot anyone who might be following her.

Get a grip, Drew, she chastised herself. Glancing at her watch, she saw that it was a quarter to twelve. Her lunch with Keith O'Brien wasn't for another fifteen minutes. She still had time to call Carla Jones, the bank teller who had testified about the account Matt had supposedly opened. Later that afternoon she hoped to talk to Peter Sands.

Stopping at a phone booth, Nancy called the bank and asked to speak with Carla Jones. The bank manager, a woman with a thin, pinched voice, informed Nancy that Carla had been on vacation in Hawaii for three weeks.

"She won a free ticket from some game show," the manager said. "She'll be back tomorrow."

Nancy was disappointed, but she had no choice but to wait. She was anxious to piece the case together as fast as possible because all her instincts told her that Matt's suspicions were well founded. She and Ned had already been threatened *and* almost run off a bridge, but so far none of her leads had given her anything to move on. She hoped her lunch with the private investigator would be more productive.

Nancy jogged back to her car and drove to the Riverside, the restaurant where she was to meet Keith O'Brien for lunch. Her spirits lifted as she approached the restaurant. The Riverside was perched high above the Muskoka River, and the view was fantastic.

When she gave her name to the maître d', he led her to a table right next to the bank of windows overlooking the river. A tall young man with dark curly hair and green eyes stood up from the table and flashed her a disarming smile. Nancy blinked when she saw him. Somehow she hadn't expected the private investigator to be so young—or so handsome.

"Hi. I'm Keith O'Brien," he said, greeting her. "It's an honor to meet you. Nancy Drew is famous in detective circles, although no one ever told me how pretty you are."

Nancy felt uncomfortable with the compliments and wanted to get right down to business. After ordering a chef's salad, she said, "Matt Goldin has asked me to look into the possibility that he was set up. I know you've already done some investigating. It would be a big help if you could tell me what you turned up."

Keith O'Brien finished buttering a roll before answering. "Well, I couldn't break the bank teller's story, if that's what you mean," he began. "If she was lying about Matt opening the account, she fooled me."

"What about Matt's suspicion of money laundering at Over the Rainbow?" Nancy asked.

"When I first read about Matt's arrest in the paper, the whole thing sounded funny to me," Keith said. "I had a feeling he was set up—that was why I went to Matt and offered him my services."

Nancy gazed at him expectantly. "And?"

"I'll tell you a secret," Keith said, after taking a bite of his roll. "I'm still on the case—I've been spending time at the Rainbow, buttering up the owner. But so far I haven't found any proof that there's money laundering going on at the club. No fake receipts, no clue as to where any illegal income might be coming from . . ." He shrugged at Nancy. "So far the place is squeaky clean."

Just then the waiter arrived with Nancy's salad and Keith's poached salmon. Nancy waited until they were alone again, then asked, "What about Bianca Engel and Tony Fry?" She told him about the conversation she and Bess had overheard, about Ned being almost run off the bridge, and about the threatening phone call she'd received.

"That does sound suspicious," Keith agreed. "Maybe I missed something."

Nancy took a sip of her ice water. "Hopefully I'll be able to collect more information. I've got a job at Over the Rainbow as a waitress. If you stop by, I'd appreciate it if you wouldn't know who I am."

"Sure thing," Keith replied. His green eyes gleamed as he added, "Say, maybe when you're done with this case, you and I can team up."

Nancy stared nervously down at her salad, stabbing at a piece of lettuce with her fork. "I already have a lot of help from my *boyfriend*," she told him, stressing the last word.

"Oh, yeah. Sure," Keith said. He backed off— for the time being. Nancy now had a feeling that working on this case was going to be even more complicated than she'd anticipated.

After leaving the Riverside, Nancy called Ned and asked him to meet her at GS Accounting Associates, so they could talk to Peter Sands. Since Ned was doing his report on Matt's case, it was important for him to be in on as much of the investigation as possible.

When she got to the small office building in downtown River Heights, Ned was waiting for her in the parking lot, his hands stuffed into the pockets of his parka. Right behind him, Nancy saw the sign marking the entrance to GS Accounting.

"Hi," Ned said, bending to kiss her lips as she came up to him.

A familiar tingle ran through her, and she realized that she wouldn't trade her boyfriend for all the Keith O'Briens in the world.

Stepping through the door to the first-floor office, Nancy and Ned found themselves in a plain, square reception area. There was no one at the front desk, but they did hear a man's voice coming from the hallway that led away from the reception area.

She shrugged at Ned, then led the way down the hallway toward the voice. Poking her head in the doorway with the voice, Nancy saw a short, stocky, blond-haired man behind a cluttered desk. He was talking on the phone, his glasses pushed up on his forehead and his tie loosened. Seeing Nancy and Ned, he waved them in. "I'll be off in a second," he mouthed silently.

While she and Ned sat down in the two leather-backed chairs facing the desk, Peter grimaced, then spoke into the receiver.

"No, Mrs. Taylor, I haven't had a chance to look over your file yet." The accountant pulled a handkerchief from his pocket and mopped his forehead with it. "I'll call you the minute I've examined the details. . . . Yes, I'm thinking of hiring someone else. . . . You'll be hearing from me soon."

No sooner did he hang up than a frantic female voice spoke up from the hall: "Peter, this is impossible—"

Nancy did a double take when she saw the dark-haired girl enter the office. It was Lisa Goldin!

Lisa was so surprised to see Nancy that she almost dropped the file she had in her hand. "Nancy! Uh, hi!" she said.

Peter focused first on Lisa, then on Nancy. "You two know each other?" he asked.

Nancy's mind was racing. What was Lisa doing helping Peter? Surely Matt must have told Lisa about his suspicions that Peter was involved in framing him. Yet she *had* been defensive of Peter at the party the night before. Why would she defend the man who may have helped send her brother to jail?

"Lisa's doing an accounting work-study program with me," Peter explained, breaking into Nancy's thoughts. From the proud expression on his face, it was obvious that Peter liked running the show at the accounting firm. When she'd swiveled around to see Lisa, Nancy noticed that the nameplate on the open door read Matt Goldin. Peter had moved into Matt's office!

"I've, uh, got to run an errand," Lisa said quickly. "Good to see you guys."

After Lisa had left, Nancy tried to explain to a distracted Peter why she and Ned had come. Nancy mentioned the possibility that Matt had been framed, and Peter became noticeably uneasy.

"Look, until I found that check I never would have thought Matt was a crook," Peter said. "But I knew there had to be a reason he was keeping me from handling his big accounts. When I found the check from Over the Rainbow I knew what that reason was."

Or perhaps Peter simply wasn't ready for the

responsibility, as Matt had claimed. Judging from the mess on his desk, he was definitely having a hard time handling the business on his own.

Nancy and Ned tried to get more detailed information about where and how Peter had found the check, or if he knew anything about a money-laundering operation, but he brushed off their questions. "Look, I have a lot of work to do. So if you wouldn't mind?" The accountant nodded toward the door.

Nancy exchanged a frustrated look with Ned. They obviously weren't going to get anything more out of Peter. Thanking him, they left the office.

"I don't know, Nan," Ned said as soon as they were outside. "Is he just totally disorganized, or is he hiding something?"

"That's the million-dollar question," Nancy told him. "And how does Lisa fit in?" She shook her head slowly. "Maybe I'll find some answers at Over the Rainbow. I'm due there in about fifteen minutes, so I'd better go." She glanced down at her black pants and white shirt, which were required attire for the comedy club's waitresses. "I'm glad I thought to put these on before I left home."

Checking his watch, Ned said, "Maybe I'll go to the library and check newspaper articles about the trial. I'll talk to you tonight."

Nancy kissed her boyfriend goodbye, then

drove to Over the Rainbow. When she walked into the comedy club, the first thing she heard was Bess's laughter. Nancy saw that Bess and Rusty were rehearsing. She couldn't hear the words, but Bess was obviously having the time of her life.

"Hey, Nancy. Catch."

Nancy turned in time to see a white apron flying toward her. She caught it just before it hit her face.

"Lesson Number One," Tony Fry said from behind the drinks counter. "Always be prepared for flying objects at a comedy club. Especially when the comics are bad."

"Thanks for the tip," Nancy said, laughing. "Where's Bianca?"

"In the office." Tony flicked a thumb toward the staircase, then turned his attention to a man wheeling a dolly loaded with cardboard cartons into the club. As Nancy started up the stairs, she heard the man call out, "Delivery."

Upstairs, a rectangle of light spilled out into the darkened hallway from an office. Nancy found Bianca behind one of two identical wooden desks that took up most of the space in the room. A large, leather-bound accounting book was open in front of her, one cover resting on the phone. As Nancy walked in, the manager rubbed her eyes and smiled.

"Hi, Nancy," Bianca said. "Glad to see you. I've got to get these books ready for the account-

ant, but I'll take you down to Jenny Reilly, the
other waitress. She'll show you the ropes."

Nancy tied on the apron Tony had thrown her
as she followed Bianca back down the stairs.
After showing Nancy where to leave her jacket
and purse, she led her to the waitress station,
near the kitchen door. A girl with short blond
hair was piling salt and pepper shakers onto a
tray.

After introducing Nancy, Bianca said, "I'm
turning the new recruit over to you, Jenny."
Then she turned and went back up the stairs.

Jenny gave Nancy an easy smile. "Boy, am I
glad to see you. It's been crazy here! Why don't
you grab some silverware and napkins, and we'll
talk as we work. Did Bianca explain how the club
works?"

"All I know is that the comedy shows are at
seven and nine, and the restaurant opens at
five-thirty," Nancy said. She smiled at Jenny. "I
guess it's up to you to tell me the rest."

"Okay, let's take it from the top." Moving over
to the tables, Jenny placed salt and pepper shakers while Nancy set out the napkins and silverware.

Nancy listened carefully as Jenny explained
how to place orders, where to pick up the food
from the kitchen and beverages from the drinks
counter, and finally where to put dirty dishes.
She and Jenny would each be responsible for half
of the restaurant's dozen tables. The job was

going to be a lot of work, Nancy realized, and it wouldn't leave much time to keep an eye on Tony and Bianca.

By the time Nancy and Jenny finished setting up, some of the comedians had begun to arrive. One of them shyly said hello to Jenny and slipped backstage. "That's Simon," Jenny told Nancy, rolling her eyes. "He's incredibly shy in real life, but on stage he's an amazing performer."

She took a pile of napkins and gestured for Nancy to sit at one of the tables at the back, near the bar. "This is the quiet before the storm," Jenny said. "If we fold these now, it'll mean one less thing to do to set up for the second show."

"How do you like working for Bianca?" Nancy asked as she reached for a napkin.

"She's okay, but she's been uptight for the past few months." Jenny lowered her voice before adding, "I'm sure you heard about the scandal with the accountant."

"I think I saw something about it in the papers," Nancy said casually. "Did you know him?"

Jenny shook her head. "No, but his junior partner used to come in pretty often to pick up the books. I think his name was Peter. He'd mostly stay at the beverage counter, talking with Tony."

Hmm, Nancy thought. Could it be that Peter had been working with Tony and Bianca to set up Matt?

Nancy was about to ask Jenny about Tony, when she saw Bianca walking toward them. "Is everything going okay?" she asked.

"Nancy's a natural," Jenny said with a grin. "We're running low on guest checks, though."

Bianca glanced toward the club's entrance, where a man in a brown uniform was waiting with a clipboard. "I have to supervise this delivery around back," she said, frowning. "The box of guest checks should be upstairs on my desk."

"I'll get it," Nancy offered quickly. With Bianca out back, she'd have a chance to snoop a little.

Bianca was already halfway out the door. "Thanks, Nancy," she called over her shoulder.

Getting up from the table, Nancy hurried toward the stairs. "Oh—excuse me," she said. She had almost run into a short man with graying dark hair coming down the stairs. Luckily, he didn't seem to mind. He just nodded and continued down the stairs.

Nancy went up the stairs and into Bianca's office. "Better find those guest checks first," she murmured to herself. She didn't see a box on Bianca's desk, but there was a small cardboard carton down by the legs of the other desk. Bending to pick it up, Nancy saw that it was taped shut. She slit open the tape with her thumbnail and opened the box.

No guest checks in here, she thought. She began idly flipping through the papers, which were receipts for various items—beverages, meat, cheese. . . .

"What's this?" she murmured out loud, staring at a receipt for sixteen cases of champagne. Over the Rainbow didn't serve alcohol, so why was there a receipt for champagne?

Nancy felt a rush of excitement as she continued flipping through the receipts. "Gaming chips —five hundred decks of cards!"

These receipts couldn't be from Over the Rainbow. They had to be from some other business, Nancy thought. Based on what she'd seen so far, it was from a *gambling* operation!

Chapter

Six

Nᴀɴᴄʏ ꜰᴇʟᴛ ᴀ ʀᴜꜱʜ as she stared at the receipts. This could be a lead—a big one!

Her mind flashed back to Dennis Lassiter's talk at the prison. He had made his money gambling and then laundered the profits by writing phony receipts to pretend he'd earned the money in his grocery business. Maybe Matt had been right, maybe the same thing was happening here. Maybe someone was running a secret gambling operation and using Over the Rainbow as a front! That was the only explanation Nancy could think of for that box of receipts.

Nancy reasoned through her theory. Someone would take these receipts, total the amounts, then create fake receipts so it looked as if the money had been spent on supplies for Over the Rainbow. The comedy club's profits would also have to be inflated, to include the amounts made from the gambling operation.

She didn't see any record of gambling profits in the box, though. A few receipts weren't proof of an illegal gambling operation, but they did give her something to go on.

Nancy took a second look at the receipt for the poker chips and cards. It was from a company called Gleason's. Fantorelli, Inc., was the name of the company on the champagne receipt. Neither company had an address listed.

If Over the Rainbow was being used to launder money, someone had to be keeping records. If she could only find them!

"Nancy? Find those checks yet?"

Nancy jumped at the sound of Jenny's voice. Her urgent gaze swept the room, landing on a box on the chair by the door. The flaps were partially open, and she could see the guest checks inside. "Yes. I'll be right down," Nancy called back.

Quickly she grabbed the tape dispenser from Bianca's desk and sealed up the box of receipts again and placed it back on the floor next to the desk. Then, taking the box of guest checks, she hurried back downstairs.

Tony glanced at her as she placed the guest checks at the waitress station. He looked as if he were going to ask her something but stopped himself as a burly man stepped into the club.

"Tony!" the man said, slapping the bartender

on the back. "Terrible weather we're having," he said in a fake British accent. "Pip, pip and all that. Cheers." The man practically bent over double in laughter.

Tony laughed politely, but Nancy thought he seemed a little nervous. "Um, hello, Johnny."

Nancy studied the man more closely. This had to be Johnny Spector, the club's owner. He was a big man with thinning gray hair, blue eyes, and a jolly red face.

"And who's this?" the man asked, turning to Nancy. "Every time I turn around, there's a new employee working for me and I'm the last one to know. I'm Johnny Spector. I own this place."

"I'm Nancy Drew," she told him. She couldn't help smiling at his flamboyant style. He acted like a character from a movie.

"Now, Nancy, don't work too hard," Johnny went on. "I like my employees to have a good time. This is a comedy club, after all. If you look unhappy, no one will laugh at any of the jokes because they'll think my waitresses hate working here. So have fun."

Nancy laughed. "Don't worry. I'm already having fun."

As Johnny continued to joke with Tony, Nancy looked around for Jenny. She didn't see her anywhere among the tables, but she did notice that several customers had been seated in her section. Nancy was about to bring them menus when the double doors to the kitchen were opened and Jenny emerged with a plate of french fries.

"I sat a party at tables three and four in your section," Jenny said. "Go get 'em, tiger."

During the next half hour the rest of Nancy's tables filled up and she was busy taking orders and delivering soft drinks. She was just bringing the first table their food when Rusty went on stage and introduced the first comedian.

"You've probably seen Bernie around town already. We're lucky to have him with us at the Rainbow tonight. Ladies and gentlemen, Bernie Weinstock!"

Nancy watched as Bernie solemnly took his place behind the microphone. He had a very whining voice and immediately started complaining about just about everything. Not everyone is a born comedian, Nancy thought to herself. But when he delivered his punchline, she couldn't help laughing out loud. His deadpan act actually turned out to be quite funny.

Glancing around the club, Nancy didn't see Bess anywhere. She was dying to tell her about the receipts. Bess was probably backstage waiting to go on. Besides, Nancy was too busy to take a break.

For the next hour or two, Nancy ran back and forth, filling food and drink orders. She didn't have a chance to observe Tony and Bianca, but from what she could tell Bianca remained up in the office most of the evening. Tony appeared to be as busy as Nancy was and didn't do anything suspicious that she could see.

Nancy was delivering sodas to one of the tables when she noticed Bianca standing next to Johnny's table. She was nodding as he talked to her, but Nancy didn't miss the frown on her face, nor the way her gaze flitted uneasily around the club. She seemed nervous—and so had Tony when Johnny first arrived earlier. Then again, if they were involved in laundering money for a gambling operation, it would make sense that they would be nervous around Johnny.

After delivering the sodas, Nancy rushed to the kitchen to pick up two dessert orders. When she returned to the floor, the entire crowd was roaring with laughter. She saw Bess and Rusty doing their sketch.

Nancy hardly recognized Bess, who was wearing a brown wig with big red bows tied around its thick braids. Bess kept interrupting Rusty, who played the lumberjack role. Nancy didn't have time to really listen to the skit, but from the loud laughter that kept ringing out, she could tell that the crowd loved Bess.

"Can a hungry man still get a burger?" a familiar voice spoke up behind Nancy as she finished delivering the desserts.

It was Keith O'Brien. Nancy felt a wave of nervousness and hoped he'd remember not to say anything to blow her cover.

Her worries disappeared a moment later. "You look new. How long have you worked here?" Keith asked innocently. Nancy saw the playful glimmer in his green eyes, but he gave no other sign that they had ever met.

"This is my first day," Nancy answered. After he gave his order, she quietly filled him in on the receipts she had found in the upstairs office. "I'm going to try to look around later for any book-keeping that indicates there really is a money-laundering operation," she concluded. In a louder voice she added, "A burger and onion rings. Will that be all?"

He nodded and Nancy went to the kitchen to place the order. A loud round of applause told her that the first show was ending. Groups of people began calling for their checks, keeping Nancy very busy.

Out of the corner of her eye, she noticed that Peter Sands had entered the club. The accountant was standing by the drinks counter, talking with Tony.

Nancy immediately turned her back to the bar. She hadn't counted on Peter showing up. If he saw her he really could blow her cover! Luckily he was so engrossed in his conversation with Tony that he didn't seem to notice anyone else.

He must have come for the accounting book, Nancy thought, recalling the ledger she'd seen Bianca working on earlier. Nancy couldn't help wondering if he had a second purpose in coming.

What if he were picking up the box of receipts from upstairs?

On the spur of the moment Nancy made a decision. She had to see the accounting book before Bianca handed it over to Peter!

Nancy was bringing change to a customer when Bess bounded toward her from backstage. "Hey, what did you think of my comedy debut?"

"You were amazing!" Nancy said, shifting her position so that her back was still to Peter and Tony. She quickly told Bess about finding the box of suspicious receipts, then explained why she didn't want the accountant to see her. "Bianca's talking to Johnny, so now's my chance to go upstairs to the office to get a look at the book."

Bess shot an appraising glance at Tony and Peter. "And you want me to keep those guys busy?"

Nancy nodded. "You guessed it. I shouldn't be more than a few minutes."

"No problem," Bess said, grinning. Nancy watched as her friend bounced over to the two guys and asked them what they thought of her act.

Nancy smiled as Tony and Peter both launched into an animated conversation with her. Way to go, Bess! After glancing over her shoulder to make sure Bianca was still talking to Johnny, Nancy walked up the stairs and into the office.

Closing the door behind her, she hurried over to Bianca's desk. The desktop was clear, so she began opening drawers, searching for the leather-bound accounting book she'd seen Bianca working on earlier. She made her way down to the bottom drawer.

"Yes!" she crowed in an excited whisper. The book was there, lying on top of some loose files. Taking it out, she placed it on the desktop and opened it.

Suddenly Nancy paused, cocking her head to one side. Was that a noise out in the hall? She tip-toed up to the door and pressed her ear against it, listening. When she didn't hear anything, she started back for the desk.

She had only gone a step or two when she heard the door swing open. Before she could turn around, she felt something hard crash down on the back of her head.

Blinding pain flashed down her spine, and Nancy's knees buckled beneath her. Then everything went black.

Chapter

Seven

OOOH . . ." Nancy's head was pounding. With a huge effort, she finally managed to open her eyes. A lot of good it did—she was staring into complete darkness.

Where was she? She felt around on the floor and pushed herself up onto her knees, then onto her feet. Groping around with her hands, she felt the solid wood of a door and something woolen brushing against her face. Stumbling over a pair of boots, Nancy realized she was in a closet.

She felt for the doorknob and was relieved when the door easily swung open. The office was empty now, Nancy saw. She took a few deep breaths to steady herself, then looked around.

"Oh, no!" she groaned, as her gaze landed on Bianca's desk. The accounting book was gone. So was the small box containing the gambling receipts.

Nancy winced as she felt the back of her head—a bump had already formed. She fought against the pain, trying to clear her head. Who could have knocked her out?

Bianca could have, but could such a petite woman have dragged her across the room to the closet? Had it been Tony? Or Peter Sands? She had to get downstairs to ask Bess if she had seen anyone go up the stairs.

Glancing at her watch, Nancy saw that she had been gone for ten minutes. Jenny was probably wondering where she was, and Bianca could return to the office at any second.

Nancy took a deep breath to steady herself, then carefully made her way back down the stairs. Tony was at the bar area, she saw, but Peter was gone. Nancy didn't see Bess, either. She must be backstage, getting ready for the second show.

As she headed back out to her station, Nancy flashed Tony a bright smile. Someone at the club was onto her, and she had no idea who it was! Her nerves were buzzing.

Nancy forced herself to concentrate on serving the customers, but her head was still throbbing. It seemed to take forever before the second show ended and the customers finally left. Then Nancy and Jenny had to put all the chairs up on the tables so the floors could be washed. It was after eleven before Nancy could take off her apron and count out her tips.

"What a night!" Bess exclaimed, appearing from backstage.

You don't know the half of it, Nancy added silently as Bess came over and sat down at the table with her and Jenny. Nancy introduced Bess to Jenny, and the girls talked about nothing in particular until Jenny said good night. As soon as she was gone, Bess leaned across the table.

"Did you get a look at the accounting book?" she asked quietly. "I'm really sorry I couldn't keep watch on Tony and Peter, but Rusty called me backstage."

Nancy glanced around to make sure no one could overhear them. When she told Bess what had happened, Bess's mouth fell open. "Nancy, you could have been seriously hurt!" she said in a horrified whisper. "I can't believe I didn't see who went upstairs. I feel awful!"

"It's not your fault," Nancy reassured her. "We'll just have to be more careful from now on. Did you get a chance to talk to any of the other comedians?"

Bess nodded. "I asked Rusty a few leading questions, but he said he was busy with the acts and never paid much attention to anything else. None of the other comedians even worked here when Matt was the accountant." Bess got up from the table and helped Nancy put the last four chairs up. "I'll keep nosing around, but I don't expect to find out much.

"Oh, one more thing," she added. "Before Rusty called me backstage, I did manage to get Peter and Tony talking about how well the club was doing. I got Tony to tell me how much he sells in drinks on an average night."

"Bess, you're incredible!" Nancy said after Bess told her the figure. "And I know how much we brought in from the food, from adding up the checks at the end of the night. If I could just get a look at that accounting book, I'd be able to see if the numbers matched up."

Nancy stifled a yawn. "Let's go home, Bess. I need a good night's sleep to think clearly about all this."

The two girls grabbed their parkas from the coat check, then said good night to Tony and Rusty, who were having a soda at the bar. Rusty gave Bess a warm hug.

"You've got real talent," he said, smiling at her.

Bess blushed and grinned back at him. "Beginner's luck," she mumbled. "But thanks for the vote of confidence. See you tomorrow."

As she and Nancy stepped out into the cold night air, Nancy raised an eyebrow at Bess. "So what's the story between you two?" she asked, zipping up her parka. "Are we talking major romance?"

"Rusty's great, but he's just-friend material,"

Bess said. She giggled, crinkling up her nose. "I'm sort of surprised to hear myself say that, but it's true."

"Well, even if he isn't going to be the love of your life, I'm glad you're having fun with him," Nancy said. "You really were great tonight. Maybe you've found your calling."

Bess rolled her eyes. "I don't think I'm cut out to be a ham all the time, but for now it's fun." She paused next to her Camaro. "So what're you going to do tomorrow?"

Nancy had just been asking herself the same question. "Well, the accounting book and receipts were up in Bianca's office," Nancy said, thinking out loud. "I didn't have much luck investigating her here. Maybe it's time to check out what she does in her free time."

"Incredible timing, Nickerson," Nancy said when she opened her front door the next morning. "Breakfast is just about ready." When she kissed him, his lips were cool from the morning's chill air.

"Mmm," Ned said. "I hope you made a lot. I'm starving."

Nancy led the way into the kitchen. As she filled both their plates with cheese omelettes, hash browns, and wheat toast, she told him about the box of receipts she'd found and about her suspicions. She also told him about the attack, glossing over it so it didn't seem serious.

"I don't like the sound of that, Nan," Ned said across the kitchen table from her. "I know that I'm not supposed to show my face at the Rainbow, but I don't like the idea of your being there alone."

"Bess is there, too," she reassured him. "Besides, I can't just back off a case, not after finding those receipts."

"Uh-oh, I know that look," Ned said skeptically. "What kind of mess are you about to get me into, Nancy?"

Nancy grinned at him. "Nothing dangerous. Just a little stakeout of Bianca Engel's apartment. I got her address from the phone book, and my binoculars are in my bag." She took a sip of her coffee. "But before we head over there I'd like to try to track down Gleason's and Fantorelli, Inc.," she added. "It's possible that they provide gambling equipment and liquor to the gambling operation."

If there is one," Ned reminded her.

When they were finished eating, Ned rinsed the dishes and loaded them into the dishwasher while Nancy checked in the phone book for the numbers for the two companies. She held a paper towel over the mouthpiece to muffle her voice, then dialed the number for Fantorelli, Inc.

Pretending to be Bianca Engel, she asked to speak with someone regarding the last order she had put in for champagne. The man on the other end of the phone didn't seem to recognize the name. When Nancy explained that perhaps Tony Fry had called in the order, she drew a blank there, too.

After she hung up, Ned tried his luck with Gleason's. He got almost the same response, although the person there did ask for an invoice and account number. Ned mumbled an excuse and hung up the phone.

"If Bianca and Tony are buying from these people, they aren't using their real names," Ned said to Nancy.

"Mmm." Checking her watch, Nancy saw that it was after nine. "I guess we should head over to Bianca's."

Ned drove to the brick apartment building near downtown River Heights where Bianca lived. Ned parked across the street, a short distance up from the building's entrance. After about twenty minutes, Nancy grabbed Ned's arm.

"We're in luck!" she said, pointing to Bianca, who was just leaving the building. She got into a sporty blue car parked in front of her building and pulled away.

"Well, she doesn't drive a white compact van," Ned commented.

"Which means someone else is probably involved," Nancy said as Ned pulled out after the blue car, keeping a safe distance between them. "Like maybe Tony Fry."

Ned sighed, keeping his eyes on Bianca's car.

"I forgot to tell you that I didn't have much luck at the library yesterday. I got a lot of background information for my project, but nothing to back up Matt's claim that he was set up *or* that there's money laundering going on at Over the Rainbow."

"Still, my hunch is that Matt is right on both counts. We just need some hard evidence," Nancy said determinedly. "Any ideas where to search for an illegal gambling operation?"

Ned shrugged. "Keep your eyes open at the club. If gambling receipts are being dropped off there, the operation could be close by."

They followed Bianca into a more residential area. When Bianca pulled into a driveway, Ned stopped about half a block away.

"She's picking up Tony," Nancy murmured as the bartender emerged from the house and slipped into the passenger side of Bianca's car.

Ned tailed them as they drove to the industrial area and stopped in front of a warehouse. He and Nancy waited for Bianca and Tony to go inside before parking across from the building. From there they could keep an eye on the entrance.

"It's Gleason's!" Ned exclaimed, pointing to the name printed on the warehouse facade.

"Let's see what they come out with," Nancy said. Now that the car had stopped and the heater was off, her hands were getting cold. She looked for her gloves, but didn't see them at first. Then she noticed they had fallen off her lap and lay wedged between the seat and door. When she opened the door to get them, the gloves fell to the ground and slid under the car. Nancy had to get out of the car to pick them up.

In that second Tony came out of the warehouse with a large cardboard box. Before Nancy could get back into the car his eyes met hers.

Nancy cringed. Tony had spotted her and there was no way she could pretend otherwise. As he took a few steps toward her, Nancy's heart stopped beating.

If Tony came over, he might recognize Ned and her cover would be blown!

Chapter

Eight

"NED! Put your head down!" Nancy whispered urgently out of the side of her mouth. "Tony spotted me."

Plastering a bright smile on her face, Nancy jogged across the street to head Tony off. "Tony. Hi!" she said brightly. "I thought I recognized you."

"Uh, hi, Nancy." Tony didn't quite meet her eyes. He shifted the cardboard box in his arms and glanced around nervously. A moment later Bianca walked out of the warehouse.

"Nancy!" Bianca said, her face going pale. "What are you doing here?"

It sounded more like an accusation than a question. "I was just out for a drive," Nancy answered vaguely. "I love this part of town—the old warehouses are so interesting. There's a lot of history here." Keeping her tone casual, she asked, "So what brings you here?"

Bianca flushed slightly. "Just some stuff for the club." Shooting a sideways glance at Tony, she added, "Well, we've got to be going. See you later."

Nancy waved to them as they got into Bianca's car and drove away. Then she poked her head into the warehouse.

"Can I help you, miss?" a gruff voice asked.

Nancy blinked until her eyes adjusted to the dim interior. A short, gray-haired man with a sour look on his face was standing about ten feet in front of her. Cardboard boxes lined the wall next to him.

"I was wondering if I could buy some cards and poker chips," Nancy said. It didn't sound believable that someone would try to buy a deck of cards at a warehouse, but the short man didn't bat an eye.

"We sell only in bulk, young lady—to companies," he said. "Sorry, but I can't help you."

Nancy thanked him, then left and crossed to Ned's sedan.

"The coast is clear," she told Ned, who was still hunched down in the driver's seat.

"What did you find out?" he asked, straightening up while Nancy got in the passenger seat.

"Nothing for sure," she replied. "But I can tell you that Gleason's definitely sells cards and poker chips. And Tony and Bianca had a big box of *some*thing. It could have been gambling stuff, which would explain why they acted so nervous."

"Right," Ned agreed. "I mean, if they were just running an errand for Over the Rainbow, there wouldn't be any reason to act so weird." He let out a low whistle. "So maybe they're in on the gambling operation!"

"We still have no concrete proof," Nancy cautioned. "Peter probably has the accounting ledger from Over the Rainbow now. Maybe we can try to sneak a peek when he goes out to lunch."

Ned checked his watch. "It's only eleven-thirty. What do you say we stop by the bank first," he suggested. "Didn't you say that the teller who testified against Matt was due back at work today?"

Fifteen minutes later Nancy and Ned were sitting in two matching leatherette chairs, waiting for the bank manager. The stern-looking, dark-haired woman bustled up to them, letting her glasses fall off her nose to her chest, where they were suspended by a silver chain.

In answer to Nancy's request to speak with Carla Jones, the bank manager pointed out a very tanned young woman with a mane of blond layers falling about her face. The young woman was lounging in one of the chairs behind the teller's windows.

"She's on break," the manager said. "I guess it's all right if you talk to her." She walked with an efficient stride over to the teller area to summon Carla, who sauntered over to Nancy and Ned and plopped down in a leatherette chair facing them. She smiled at Ned.

"The manager said you guys wanted to ask me something?" Carla said, pulling a candy bar out of her purse. "I've only got a few minutes left on my break. Anybody want a piece?"

"No, thanks," Nancy and Ned said at the same time.

Nancy got straight to the point. "Carla, I was wondering if you could tell me about the account you opened for Matt Goldin."

"Oh, not this again," Carla said, frowning. "He came in and opened an account under the name Gold Enterprises. He signed a signature card and deposited one check." She sounded as if she were reciting a shopping list, not talking about events that had put a man behind bars.

"And you identified him at the trial?" Nancy probed.

"Yes, I did," Carla said. "Smallish guy, with a beard."

She wasn't exactly bursting with information, Nancy noticed. Was that because she had something to hide?

"You must have handed him a deposit record for the check, right?" Nancy said. She was hoping that the more detailed her questions were, the more likely that Carla would get nervous—if she was lying.

"Look, we went through all this at the trial," Carla said abruptly. "Now if you'll excuse me, I have to get back to work."

"Sure," Nancy said pleasantly. "Oh, by the way, how was Hawaii?" If Carla wouldn't talk about Matt's account, perhaps she'd give away information about who had arranged her trip.

The teller's expression immediately softened. "Oh, it was great. Three whole weeks, all expenses paid. I wish I could have stayed forever."

Ned smiled. "Maybe you'll get another chance."

"No, the trip was a gift from my uncle. I don't think you get that kind of present twice." With that, Carla walked back to her teller station.

"That's strange," Nancy said, turning to Ned. "Yesterday on the phone the bank manager told me that Carla had won the trip, but Carla just said that her uncle paid for it."

"I guess somebody got the story wrong," Ned said with a shrug.

"Or Carla got a free trip to Hawaii for lying at a trial," Nancy speculated.

"You don't have any proof of that," Ned pointed out.

"Not yet," Nancy answered. "Not yet."

* * *

"It's after twelve-thirty," Ned said as he pulled up outside the GS Accounting office. "Do you think Peter's gone to lunch?"

Nancy grabbed Ned's arm. "There's our answer," she whispered, nodding toward the door. Peter Sands was just leaving the office.

They hunched down in Ned's car, watching as Peter climbed into a Geo and drove away.

"We're in luck," Ned said as he and Nancy made their way toward the entrance.

Through the glass window, Nancy could see the receptionist at her desk, reading a magazine. "What are we going to do about her?" she murmured.

"Never fear," Ned said, grinning at her. He looked at the businesses and restaurants near where GS Accounting Associates was located. "The Nickerson charm is about to pay off. I'll bet anything she won't be able to resist the opportunity to have a quick soda with a charming guy like me—at that luncheonette," he added, pointing across the street.

Nancy giggled. "You gigolo," she teased. "Okay, I'll wait in the car."

Sure enough, a few minutes later, Ned and the receptionist emerged from the building. As soon as they went into the luncheonette, Nancy hurried to the GS Accounting Associates office. Pulling her lock-pick from her bag, she went to work on the door. Within a minute the lock had clicked open and she slipped inside, turning the deadbolt behind her.

In Peter's office the desk was still piled as high with papers as it had been the day before. It took Nancy a few moments before she spotted Over the Rainbow's accounting book. Next to it was a pile of files, the top one labeled, 'Rainbow: Travel Receipts.'

Nancy flipped open the manila file folder. Inside were various hotel receipts and a receipt for an airline ticket. Studying the receipt, she saw that it had been issued to J. Spector. The destination was Hawaii.

A small shiver ran down her spine. The departure date was three weeks before—about the time Carla Jones had left on her vacation to Hawaii! Clipped to the ticket was confirmation of a hotel reservation under the same name, at a hotel on Maui, one of the islands making up Hawaii. Was she holding the receipt of the ticket Carla had used for her trip?

Hold it, Nan, she cautioned herself. Maybe Johnny had used the ticket himself. When she checked the return flight from Hawaii, she saw that it was for the day before. Nancy hadn't noticed a tan when she saw Johnny at the comedy club the night before. No one at Over the Rainbow had mentioned that he had been out of town, either, nor did he mention it himself. That definitely seemed out of character for him.

He probably would have mentioned a trip to Hawaii.

Nancy thought hard. She could call the hotel and get them to describe J. Spector. If they described a woman like Carla, then Nancy could be almost positive that someone had bought Carla a free trip to Hawaii, using Johnny's name and the Over the Rainbow account.

The question was, who could have arranged the trip? Peter and Bianca seemed the likeliest suspects, since they had free access to the book. And since Tony and Bianca seemed to be up to something, the bartender could be involved, too.

Nancy frowned as she considered another possibility. What if Johnny himself had arranged the trip for Carla? After all, the ticket was in his name and he *was* the owner of Over the Rainbow. He might have had a hand in framing Matt. That would mean that he was probably also involved in any gambling or money laundering that was going on.

Still, Matt had said that he was more of a figurehead than anything else. He didn't give the impression that he paid any attention to the business end of the club. If Johnny were involved in anything illegal, Nancy didn't see why Bianca and Tony would be so nervous around him.

Nancy was deep in thought as she slipped the ticket back into the folder. She was just opening the heavy leather accounting book when the office door flew open.

Nancy's heart leapt to her throat when she saw the dark-haired girl in the doorway. It was Lisa Goldin. Lisa planted her hands on her hips and glared at Nancy with cold, dark eyes.

"What do you think you're doing here, Nancy?"

Chapter

Nine

NANCY'S HEART POUNDED against her chest. She hadn't counted on Lisa's being in the office. How am I going to get out of this one? her mind screamed. I've been caught red-handed!

Thinking fast, Nancy decided to try to turn the tables on Lisa. "Actually, I wanted to ask you the same question," Nancy said forcefully. "Why are you working with Peter when he could be the person who framed your brother?"

Lisa blinked, momentarily stunned. Then her whole body slumped forward. She sank into a chair next to Peter's desk and buried her head in her hands. When she finally looked at Nancy, her brown eyes were glistening with tears.

"Peter and I had just started dating when Matt was first arrested," she began in a small voice. "I really like him a lot."

79

So *that* was why Lisa was so defensive of Peter, Nancy realized. That still didn't explain what she was doing here, though.

"When it first came out that Peter was the one who'd found the canceled check that Matt supposedly deposited in that fake account. . . ." Lisa took a deep breath and let it out slowly. "Well, I didn't want to believe that Peter had helped set him up, even though a little voice kept nagging at me."

"So you decided to help out here so you could find out for yourself," Nancy guessed.

Lisa nodded. "Besides, look at this place!" she exclaimed, gesturing around the messy office. "Peter can't handle it all on his own. The business is falling apart. The least I can do is try to help Matt hold on to it, so something will be left when he gets out."

"Have you found any evidence that Peter *did* help set up Matt?" Nancy asked gently.

"No." Lisa seemed both sad and relieved. "Peter's been very protective of the bigger accounts—the ones Matt wouldn't let him handle before. Every time I offer to help him, he brushes me off. The truth is, I haven't been able to examine Over the Rainbow's records yet. Today I made sure he had a lunch appointment so that I could take a look at them."

"Take a look at what?"

Nancy and Lisa both whirled around as Peter Sands walked into the office.

"Peter! What are you doing back from lunch already?" Lisa asked, her hands flying to her face.

"I forgot a file." Peter pushed his glasses up on his nose, then paused, staring first at Nancy, then at the open ledger on the desk in front of her. "What's going on here?" he asked, his eyes narrowing.

Suddenly Lisa burst into tears. "I—I think you may have s-set up Matt!" she stammered.

"What are you talking about?" Peter asked, a shocked look in his eyes.

"You were the one who found the canceled check that led the police to that fake account," Lisa said, wiping her eyes. "Matt said he never saw the check and didn't go anywhere near the bank. I believe him!"

"I know that's what he said. Don't you think I wanted to believe him?" Peter asked.

Stepping in, Nancy said, "Maybe you'd better tell us exactly what happened, Peter."

Peter leaned against the edge of his desk and crossed his arms over his chest. "I found the canceled check by accident. It was mixed in with a bunch of checks and papers from an account of mine. I don't know how it got there. Maybe I should have asked Matt about it before I investigated myself, but I just thought he was hiding something from me."

So far this fit with what Nancy knew already. "Go on," she encouraged.

"The check was from Over the Rainbow's

account, and it was made out to Gold Enterprises," Peter continued. "It had Matt's signature. You see, he was allowed to sign checks for the club for amounts up to ten thousand dollars. The weird thing was that Gold Enterprises was what Matt had wanted to call our company, instead of GS Accounting."

"So that made you suspicious of Matt?" Nancy asked Peter.

"Sure. Then I found out that Gold Enterprises was Matt's company—so I blew the whistle on him."

Lisa had been listening silently to Peter's explanation. "But how did that canceled check get into your file?" she asked him now. "I mean, if my brother really was stealing money from the Rainbow, wouldn't he be extra careful?"

"Yeah, I guess," Peter answered with a shrug. "But even careful people can make mistakes."

That was possible, Nancy supposed. It was also possible that someone *else* had placed that check in Peter's file on purpose, so Peter would find it. Of course, whoever might have done that would have to know about the bad feelings between the two partners.

"Peter, did anybody besides Lisa know about the trouble between you and Matt?" Nancy asked.

Peter thought for a moment. "I complained to Tony about it sometimes, when I picked up the accounting book. But that's all." All at once Peter understood what Nancy was implying. "You don't really think someone planted that check for me to find, do you?"

When Nancy didn't say anything, Peter shook his head. "You have no proof that that's what happened."

Nancy had to admit he was right. Somewhere she was just going to have to find proof.

"Look, let's continue this later," Peter said, checking his watch. "I'm already late for my lunch meeting."

After he'd left, Lisa turned worried eyes on Nancy. "Do you think he's telling the truth?"

Before Nancy could answer, Ned walked in. He was surprised to see Lisa there. "What happened?" he asked. "When the receptionist and I returned I saw Peter leaving."

"I'll explain later," Nancy said. Turning to Lisa, she said, "In answer to your question, my guess is that Peter *is* telling the truth. He seemed sincere, but we can't be sure without proof. Let's take a look at Over the Rainbow's accounting ledger. But first I want to make a quick call to Hawaii."

Ned raised an eyebrow. "Is this a little surprise vacation for two?"

"I wish," Nancy said, grinning. She told him and Lisa about the airline receipt that she had found in Over the Rainbow's travel file. "I'm going to call the hotel and ask them to describe the person who checked in under the name

Spector," she concluded. "Hopefully it's not a big hotel and they'll know who I'm talking about."

Nancy dialed the number on the hotel confirmation notice and asked for the front-desk manager. "Hello," she said into the phone in her best official-sounding voice. "Did you have a Mr. or Miss Spector staying with you recently?"

Nancy waited while she was put on hold. A moment later the manager came back on the line. "There was a Miss J. Spector here," he said. "She checked out yesterday."

When Nancy asked the manager if he could describe Miss Spector, he said, "Oh, she was a pretty young girl—cascades of blond hair cut in layers. I remember because she had me find a stylist to give her a trim while she was here."

That definitely sounded like Carla Jones, Nancy thought. Now she just needed to know one more thing. "I'm calling from her business accounting office," she explained. "We wanted to make sure that her account was paid for by the firm. Could you check on that, please?"

She could barely contain her excitement when she hung up a few moments later.

"Well?" Ned asked.

"Her bill was paid by a check from Over the Rainbow!" Nancy said.

Lisa's mouth fell open. "If they paid for her trip to Hawaii, that makes her testimony at Matt's trial a little shaky."

"More than a little," Nancy said. "But we need more. If Matt didn't open the Gold Enterprises account or sign the check, someone else did a very good job of forging his signature—good enough to fool two experts. We have to find out who that person is."

Ned raked a hand through his thick brown hair. "And since all our suspects work at Over the Rainbow, we also have to have solid proof that there really was a money-laundering operation going on, as Matt claimed."

"I say we start by taking a look at this book while we have the chance," Lisa said, leaning forward to look at the Over the Rainbow ledger.

The three of them started poring over the leather-bound book. "Based on what Bess found out from Tony, and from what I calculated from last night's guest checks, the club's average take per night is around five thousand dollars," Nancy said.

Lisa ran her fingers down the entries for each day's profits. "These records definitely show more income than that per night," she said. "They show closer to *ten* thousand dollars, sometimes more."

Two piles of receipts were wedged into the book. Ned took them out and glanced at them. "Hmm, looks like these are the guest receipts and totals from the bar," he said. "And this other stack is of bills that Over the Rainbow needs to pay out." He reached for the calculator on Peter's desk. "I'll add these up to make sure the numbers match."

A moment later he held up a slip of paper, frowning at it. "Check it out. This company is getting a nice payment—almost five thousand dollars."

"What company is that?" Nancy asked, leaning over Ned's shoulder.

"Allen Associates," Ned told her. "The payment is listed as a consulting fee."

Lisa flipped back a few pages in the accounting book. "They get about the same amount every month! Nancy, do you think this could be a bogus payment?"

"Maybe," Nancy said. "It's certainly something to check out."

Ned copied the name and address from the receipt. "Definitely," he agreed. "I'll track down Allen Associates myself. But first I think we could use some lunch. Pizza at Palsson's?"

Nancy smiled up at him. "Great idea! I'll see if Bess can meet us there."

Bess held a piece of hot, cheesy pizza high over her plate. A single string of cheese stretched between the slice and the pie on the table.

"Anybody want to place bets on how high I can lift this slice before the cheese snaps?" Bess asked, laughing.

Nancy grinned at her friend. "No bets, please

—not when we're trying to track down an illegal gambling operation," she teased.

Ned took a huge bite of his slice, then washed it down with some soda. "I've been thinking about those receipts you saw, Nan, the ones for cards and chips and champagne. I think we should try to find out where this gambling is taking place."

"If you were a gambling operation, where would you be?" Bess asked.

Nancy slowly pushed aside her slice of pizza. "You know Caribou, that dance club around the corner from the Rainbow? It seems like a hangout for teens, but I've seen older people go in there, too."

Bess snapped her fingers. "Right! Like that couple we saw the other night. It doesn't make sense that they'd go to a dance club that plays rock music and only has a juice bar," she said, giggling.

"Hmm," Ned said. "It's worth checking out. Maybe you two should go to the club tonight after you get off work."

"Sounds good to me," Bess said. "That's the kind of investigating I like. Yikes!" Bess exclaimed, looking at her watch. "I'm supposed to be at Over the Rainbow in ten minutes to rehearse with Rusty."

After Bess left, Nancy turned her full attention to Ned. "I'm already dressed for work, but I don't have to be there for over an hour," she said.

"What do you say we go back to my house to relax?"

"Good idea," he agreed. "I feel as if my mind is on overload."

As Ned drove toward her house, Nancy's mind sorted through all they'd learned. "Tonight I'm going to search the office again for some concrete proof that Over the Rainbow is laundering money for a gambling operation."

Nancy paused, glancing out the windshield at the passing traffic. She blinked as something caught her eye.

"Ned! Look at the van that's just passing us!" she exclaimed, pointing through the windshield. "It's the same one that tried to run us off the bridge!"

Chapter

Ten

A<small>RE YOU SURE</small> it's the same one?" Ned asked, peering straight ahead. He gripped the steering wheel tightly.

"Positive," Nancy replied. "I saw the twisted bumper and the blue stripe as it was passing us. Whatever you do, don't lose it!"

They followed the white compact van to an industrial area. It pulled to a stop outside a warehouse dotted with small windows. Ned stopped next to the curb a short distance away.

Nancy did a double take when she saw a small man with graying dark hair get out of the van and slam the door behind him.

"Hey, that's the same guy I saw at the comedy club, right before I found that box of receipts!" she exclaimed. "I wonder if he was there to drop off the box. I practically ran into him on the stairs. If he got suspicious, he could have followed me back upstairs and knocked me out."

She and Ned watched as the man went into the warehouse. A moment later he came out and peered up and down the street before motioning to someone inside. Two beefy guys appeared pushing a handcart with two felt-covered tables loaded on top.

Nancy took her binoculars out of her purse and focused on the tables. She could see little card squares etched in the felt. "I can't tell whether those tables are for poker or blackjack, but they're definitely gambling tables!" she said triumphantly.

After the tables were loaded into the back of the van, the two men went back into the warehouse. This time they returned with the top of a roulette wheel.

"Bingo!" Ned said under his breath. "They're taking a big chance loading this stuff in daylight."

Nancy continued to look through the binoculars. "It's not illegal to make or ship gambling equipment. They could say they're shipping it to Las Vegas or Atlantic City. Gambling is legal there."

"That's true," Ned agreed with a nod. "But I doubt that van is going to either of those places. I'll bet anything this van is heading to a gambling site right here in River Heights!"

Nancy watched as the two guys slammed the

van doors. Then she lowered the binoculars. The small man with the graying hair practically vaulted into the driver's seat and pulled the van in a tight U-turn. Ned let him get a short distance ahead before following.

"He's turning," Nancy said a few minutes later. Ned followed, but Nancy was dismayed that the street they turned into was thick with traffic. Up ahead, the van accelerated through a yellow light.

"I can't make that light," Ned groaned, hitting his hand against the steering wheel.

"I can still see him up ahead," Nancy said. "He's making a right!"

After the light changed to green, Ned still had to switch lanes. By the time he made the right, then tried to pick up speed, the compact van was nowhere in sight.

"Sorry, Nan," Ned said, letting out a disappointed sigh.

"Oh well. We tried," she answered, trying to sound more cheerful than she felt.

"Wait, I have an idea." Ned's brown eyes suddenly shone excitedly. "Let's go back to the warehouse and pretend that we're with the guy in the van. We could say that he forgot something and try to sneak a look at the address on the order form."

Nancy straightened up. "Ned, you're brilliant!"

Ned circled back to the warehouse. "Maybe I

should talk to them," he suggested, pulling his car to a halt in front of the warehouse. "They'll be more likely to think that a big hulking guy like me would be in on this delivery than a beautiful, incredibly smart redhead."

"I think that was a compliment," Nancy said, leaning over to plant a kiss on his cheek. "Okay, you win. I'll watch from the car."

Nancy hunched down in her seat and watched through the rearview mirror as Ned went inside the warehouse. A minute later he came back out and hurried to the sedan.

"I should be an actor," he said, slipping in behind the wheel and starting the car.

"What did you find out?" Nancy asked.

"I found the foreman and told him that we forgot the bottom of the roulette table. He seemed pretty confused. Then he checked the order and said that we already had the bottom. So I told him, well, somebody's got it wrong."

Nancy grinned at him. "And you just happened to sneak a peek at the address on the order form?" she guessed.

"You got it," he said proudly.

When he repeated the address to her, Nancy's eyes widened. "That's on the same street as Over the Rainbow. It's probably too late to catch them unloading the van, though. I can check the address when I get to work."

Ned glanced at his watch. "Speaking of work,

don't you have to be at the club? It's twenty-five to four."

"What time does the bank close?" she asked.

"Four, I think. Why?"

Nancy had a glint in her eye. "I'd like to pay another visit to our friend Carla Jones. If we confront her with the things we've guessed about her vacation, she just might crack."

"Good idea, Drew," Ned said. "I have a feeling that her tan is going to start peeling when she sees us again."

By the time Nancy and Ned arrived at the North Central Bank, it was a quarter to four. This time Carla Jones spotted them as they sat down to wait. Nancy carefully watched her face, which visibly paled beneath its tan.

Carla still had a couple of customers to finish with before walking over to join Ned and Nancy. From the wary expression on her face, Nancy could tell that Carla wasn't pleased to see them.

"Listen, I have a lot to do. I don't have time to talk to you," Carla said, before Nancy even opened her mouth. "Besides, I don't have anything more to say."

"We won't keep you long, Carla," Nancy pressed. "It's just that I'm a little confused about that trip you took. Your manager said you won the trip, but you told us that your uncle paid for it."

Ned stared straight into Carla's eyes. "And then we were going through some accounts at Over the Rainbow and I found your ticket," he added.

"That's impossible," Carla snapped. "You couldn't trace that ticket to me—it didn't even have my name on it."

Carla gasped as she realized her mistake, then focused on the floor.

"Do you admit that someone from Over the Rainbow paid for your trip to Hawaii?" Nancy pressed her advantage.

"I admit I went to Hawaii," Carla mumbled, still not raising her head. "As far as I know, it's perfectly legal to take a vacation."

"Lying on the witness stand is a federal crime, Carla," Nancy said solemnly. "You could be in big trouble if you don't cooperate."

There was a long pause before Carla finally looked back up at Nancy and Ned. "Am I—am I in big trouble?" she asked, her voice a whisper.

"That depends," Ned put in. "If you tell us the truth now and help us find out who framed Matt Goldin, the court will take that into consideration. You might get off easier."

Carla sat down heavily on the leatherette chair next to Ned. "I agreed to lie on the witness stand in exchange for the trip," she stated flatly. "I knew it was wrong, but they made the trip sound so terrific and I couldn't have afforded any kind of vacation this year."

Tears were beginning to well up in the teller's eyes. Nancy opened her purse and pulled out a small package of tissues, handing Carla one. "Who was 'they'?" Nancy asked.

Carla shrugged. "A guy—I don't know who. We made all the arrangements over the phone."

"Did he have a British accent?" Ned asked, leaning forward.

"No, I'm sure he wasn't British," Carla replied firmly.

Nancy thought back to her conversation with Tom Irwin, Matt's lawyer. "You testified that Matt opened that account. You even identified him in court. What really happened?"

"A man did come in and open an account for Gold Enterprises. He deposited a check, too," Carla said. She lowered her eyes before adding, "It wasn't Matt, though."

"Who was it? What did he look like?" Ned asked.

"I don't know. He kept his sunglasses and a hat on the whole time. He didn't have a beard, so I knew he wasn't Matt."

"Do you think you'd recognize the man if you saw him again?" Nancy asked Carla.

"Maybe," the teller replied. "People come in every day and open accounts, but he did have a striking face, even with his sunglasses on. I might recognize him."

Nancy was disappointed not to get a better description of the person, but at least she now had proof that Matt had been framed. "Are you willing to tell Matt's lawyer this?" she asked.

"Yes," Carla said emphatically. "I haven't been able to live with myself ever since this happened. I didn't even have a good time in Hawaii. The whole thing was a big mistake."

"Thanks, Carla," Nancy said with a smile. "I'll be sure to tell Matt's lawyer how helpful you've been."

Nancy and Ned were silent as they left the bank and got back into Ned's car. Ned waited until he pulled out into the late-afternoon traffic before speaking.

"You were right on that one, Nancy. Matt really was framed," he said.

"Whoever opened the account in his name must have forged his signature," Nancy added. She folded her arms across her chest. "We know Bianca didn't open the account, since it was a man."

"But Tony could have," Ned put in. "Or even that guy we saw in the van today."

"I'll see what I can find out tonight at work," Nancy said.

Nancy was late for work when Ned pulled into the parking lot of Over the Rainbow.

"I'm just going to check on that address quickly before I start my shift," she said. "I'll call you when I get home if we turn up anything at Caribou later."

Ned leaned over to give her a long, lingering kiss. "Just be careful," he said gruffly. "Meanwhile I'll follow up on Allen Associates. I'll let you know the second I find out anything."

After Ned drove away, Nancy walked over to the entrance to Caribou. Sure enough, the address matched the one Ned had seen on the delivery order.

It was still early. The dance club's neon sign was dark and window blinds were drawn. There was no sign of the white van. Nancy walked up to the heavy, tinted-glass door and cupped her hands around her eyes to see better into the darkness.

All of a sudden Nancy was struck by the feeling that someone was watching her. The next thing she knew, a heavy hand had clamped down on her shoulder.

Chapter

Eleven

NANCY SPUN AROUND with a gasp. The sun, low in the western sky, blinded her, so at first she didn't recognize the man standing in front of her.

"Keith," she said, trying not to betray her nervousness. "What are you doing here?"

"Just out for a walk," he said, giving her a warm smile. "I see you're curious about this place, too. I always hear good music pounding out, but I haven't had a chance to come here yet."

There was something about his explanation that was too smooth. "How's the investigation going?" she asked, watching him closely.

Keith laughed. "Nothing new on my end. I was just going to ask you the same question."

"I don't have any solid proof," she answered vaguely. She wasn't sure why, but her instincts told her to keep quiet about Carla and her suspicions that Over the Rainbow was inflating its profits and expenses.

Nancy glanced down in order to avoid Keith's probing green eyes. "Oh—I'm really late," she said, gesturing at her watch. "I'll catch up with you later."

Before he could say anything, Nancy turned and walked hurriedly toward the entrance to the comedy club. She hadn't considered Keith a suspect before.

Now that she thought about it, though, Keith could have been the one who'd knocked her out in the office the night before. She had told him that she was going to snoop around up there. And that phone call she'd received at Tom Irwin's office—that was right after she'd made her lunch date with Keith. She vaguely recalled telling him about her plans to visit the lawyer's office.

Nancy mentally shook herself. She couldn't prove anything without solid proof, and that, unfortunately, was one thing she didn't have yet.

Hurrying into the comedy club, Nancy found Bianca setting up the tables with Jenny. "I'm so sorry I'm late," Nancy said breathlessly.

Bianca didn't quite meet Nancy's eyes. Her manner was stiff, almost cold. "That's all right. You're here now." She handed over the pile of silverware she had been placing on the tables. "Why don't you finish up here." With that the manager headed for the stairs at the rear of the club.

"Talk about a cool reception," Nancy murmured under her breath, following Bianca with her eyes. Was it just because she was late, or was it possible that Bianca knew about her investigation? After their meeting at Gleason's, Bianca might have become suspicious.

Jenny was setting up tables at the opposite end of the club. Nancy waved to her, shrugged out of her jacket, and got to work.

"Hi, Nancy," Bess greeted Nancy a moment later, jumping off the stage and coming over to the table Nancy was setting. "I was afraid you weren't going to make it today."

"I got held up," Nancy explained. In an undertone, she told Bess about following the van and about her run-in with Keith outside the dance club. "I guess we'd better keep an eye on him tonight if we see him, as well as on Bianca and Tony," she finished.

"Sounds good," Bess agreed. "Nancy, if that stuff was delivered to Caribou, then maybe there really *is* gambling there."

Nancy shrugged. "Hopefully we'll find out after we get off work tonight." She nodded toward one of the tables near the bar, where Rusty and Johnny were sitting. Loud laughter rang out from the table. "After finding that ticket with Johnny's name on it, we can't rule Johnny out as a suspect, either," she added.

"I'll keep an eye on him," Bess promised. "Actually, Rusty told me that Johnny used to be a pretty famous comedian in the old days. I think he might even do a little stand-up comedy tonight."

Just then Rusty got up from the table and gestured to Bess, before heading toward the stage. "Oops, duty calls," Bess told Nancy.

"How's the routine going?" Nancy asked.

"I'm having a lot of fun, but it's not like it's my life's career or anything." With a smile, she hurried backstage after Rusty.

As Nancy finished setting up, she glanced around the room. Tony was busy behind the bar, cutting up lemons and limes. Bianca wasn't in sight, so Nancy assumed she was still up in her office.

Nancy had just finished placing the last piece of silverware when Keith walked into the club. He sat down on one of the barstools and began talking to Tony. As Nancy walked by on her way to the waitress station, he smiled and said, "Tony tells me Johnny might be performing tonight."

"So I hear," Nancy said politely. "I wonder what his jokes are like."

Keith chuckled to himself. "Oh, he's a riot, all right. I've known him for a few years now, and he always manages to bring down the house."

"Um, yeah, sure." Nancy was barely listening. The club was beginning to fill up, and she was too busy now to pay any attention to Keith or to think about the case.

Before long Rusty went on stage to introduce

the opening act. "I've got a surprise for you tonight. How many of you remember Johnny Spector? Well, he owns the Rainbow, and it's been too long since he's graced the stage with his presence. So please give a warm welcome to the Big Guy himself—Mr. Johnny Spector!"

The crowd broke into wild cheering. Johnny's style was different from that of the younger comedians. He delivered a lot of one-liners, instead of telling stories or doing impressions, but Nancy had to admit he was funny. The crowd loved him.

As Nancy came out of the kitchen after placing a food order, Tony gestured to her. His hand was cupped over the telephone receiver, which he waved at her.

"It's for you."

Hurrying over to the bar, she took the phone from him. "Hello?"

"It's me."

It was Ned, and Nancy knew he wouldn't call her at work unless it was important. "Hi! How are you?" she said brightly. She shot a nervous glance at Tony, who was already busy at the far end of the counter. Keith was only a few feet away, though, so she had to be careful.

"Remember those payments to Allen Associates, the consulting firm? I found something very interesting," Ned said.

"What?" Nancy asked, her tone and her expression casual.

"I traced the address on the receipt, and it's an empty lot. There is no such thing as Allen Associates," Ned's excited voice came back on the line.

Nancy was about to ask him if he'd found out who had created the company, when she heard a faint click over the line.

Someone was listening in on their conversation!

Chapter

Twelve

NANCY HAD to get off the phone before Ned revealed anything more!

"Um, listen, it's really busy here. I have to go, okay?" Without waiting for an answer, she hung up.

Nancy's whole body filled with dread as she scanned the room. Who had been listening in?

Tony was behind the bar, and there wasn't another extension there that he could have picked up. Keith was still sitting near Nancy—he couldn't have picked up an extension either.

Nancy looked up as Bianca walked down the stairs. The manager glanced briefly at Nancy, then went into the kitchen. It had to have been her, Nancy reasoned. Tony could have alerted her about Nancy's call before he handed Nancy the phone. Bianca could have been listening on the extension in her office!

"Nancy, you've got three or four orders up," Jenny called over to her, hurrying past with two plates.

Nancy sighed and headed for the kitchen. She picked up three dinner plates filled with food, balancing them on her hands and arms, then hurried to her tables. After serving the food, she glanced at her watch.

She had a fifteen-minute break coming up after the next comedian. The way things were going, she didn't want to wait until the end of her shift to check out the dance club. If someone was onto her, she had to get over there before anyone got to her! Maybe she could slip out on her break and check around for the gambling operation.

As Nancy returned to the bar to pick up a drinks order, she noticed that Keith was leaving. He'd gotten up from the bar and was standing next to the door talking to Johnny. They laughed uproariously about something. Then Johnny slapped Keith on the back, and Keith left. She wished she could follow him, but she couldn't leave.

"Tony, I have to talk to you for a minute." Bianca's stern voice interrupted Nancy's thoughts. "Look at these and tell me what you think."

Bianca had stepped up to the counter. Nancy

couldn't believe it when she saw what the assistant manager was holding. It was a cardboard box the exact same size as the one in which Nancy had found the gambling receipts the night before!

Nancy didn't want to call attention to herself, so she hunched over the counter, pretending to add up some checks. She watched out of the corner of her eye as Bianca opened the box and took out a piece of paper. Nancy's heart started pounding. Was Bianca showing Tony one of the gambling receipts?

"I don't think that works," Tony said, frowning at the paper.

"Do you think it's too much?" Bianca asked.

Tony shook his head. "No. We've got to make it look real."

What was going on? It sounded to Nancy as if they were talking about faking the accounting books, right out in the open!

Suddenly Tony's expression became guarded. "Bianca, put it away," he said under his breath. "Johnny's coming."

Nancy glanced back over her shoulder and saw Johnny approaching the bar.

Bianca quickly slipped the paper back in the box and closed the lid. "Uh, hi, Johnny," she said nervously. "You were great up there."

"Thanks. It felt good," Johnny said too loud. "I haven't been on a stage in a long time."

"You should do it more often," Tony told him, forcing a grin. "You really brought the house down."

Bianca chimed in, "We should make you a regular act, Johnny. Why don't you talk to Rusty about it?"

"Nah, you kids want to hear the new comics. I just do the old material. I'm like a dinosaur around here," Johnny said, but Nancy noticed that he was pleased by the compliment. "Hey, Tony. How about a cold soda?"

He waved to someone across the club. "I see another old dinosaur. Thanks for the soda," Johnny said, taking the glass Tony offered him. "Keep up the good work."

Tony and Bianca smiled stiffly as Johnny walked over to his friend. As soon as he was out of earshot, they both sighed out loud.

"He didn't see anything, did he?" Bianca asked worriedly.

"No, but I thought all this craziness would be over by now," Tony said. "I've been jumping out of my skin for weeks!"

He stiffened as his gaze lit on Nancy. "What can I get you, Nancy?" he asked, suddenly businesslike.

"Um, two ginger ales, Tony," she told him. She wished she could peek at what was in the box, but Bianca had closed it. With a sigh, Nancy returned to her work.

After she had delivered her sodas, Nancy saw that it was time for her break. She told Jenny to cover for her, then got her leather jacket from the coat check and hurried outside.

The cold air felt refreshing as she walked the short distance to Caribou. Although the two buildings were connected, they had separate entrances. When Nancy opened the door to the dance club, she could hardly believe how loud the music was. A beefy guy wearing jeans, a black shirt, and a leather vest stood next to the door. Behind him, Nancy saw a dim, cavernous room. Colored lights strobed over the crowd of people filling the dance floor.

"Ten bucks to get in," the guy at the door told her.

Nancy flashed him her brightest smile. "I just wanted to look around," she said, shouting so he could hear her over the music. "My friends and I are thinking about renting this space for a party."

The beefy guy hesitated, then yelled back, "Okay. You can look around, but don't let me catch you in there dancing." He grinned, showing off two gold teeth.

Nancy started to move past him, then paused. "Are there other rooms besides the big club space?" she asked.

"Sure, we have two rooms you can rent for private parties upstairs," he said loudly, gesturing toward a staircase that rose up to the right, behind him. "But you can't go up there now. They're rented."

"Oh, okay," Nancy said. She was relieved when a couple came in the door behind her, and the doorman turned his attention to them. Stepping behind him, Nancy quickly slipped up the stairs.

She found herself at one end of a long hallway. At the far end was a man in a tuxedo, standing in front of a door, a clipboard in his hand.

Seeing a rest room near the top of the stairs, Nancy ducked into it. Luckily it was empty. If there *was* gambling going on in that room, she reflected, the guy with the clipboard probably wasn't going to let just anybody in. She had to figure out a way to get past him.

Nancy perched next to the rest-room door, opening it just a crack to peer out. Before long, a well-dressed couple came up the stairs. It sounded as if the woman was complaining about the music.

"As if we don't hear enough of that rubbish coming from Andrew's room," she snorted.

Nancy smiled to herself. That was pretty much how her father felt about her music. The couple gave their names to the tuxedoed man, and he opened the door for them.

Another couple quickly followed the first.

"Name, please?" the doorman asked.

"Pierson," the man said.

"Oh, look, James," the woman said, peeking over the doorman's shoulder at his clipboard. "Michelle Foley is coming tonight."

"I'm sorry, ma'am, but you're not supposed to see the list," the tuxedoed man told her.

"Of course," the woman said graciously. "You're just doing your job."

After the couple disappeared into the room, Nancy took a deep breath. If she was ever going to see what was behind that door, it would have to be now.

She closed the rest-room door and quickly applied fresh blusher and lip gloss. She wasn't as dressed up as the women she'd just seen, but with her jacket closed, she looked like she had on a fancier outfit than just waitressing clothes. Holding her chin high, she stepped out of the rest room and walked confidently up to the doorman.

"Michelle Foley," Nancy announced in a clipped voice. "Are the Piersons here yet?"

The doorman didn't even bat an eye. "Just came in. Have a nice evening, Ms. Foley."

He opened the door and Nancy stepped inside. After moving down a hallway, she emerged into a large, open room—and stopped short.

Nancy couldn't believe her eyes. Slot machines stretched along the wall on her left. Crowds milled around poker tables and blackjack tables, and the roulette wheel was spinning.

It was a full-blown casino!

Chapter

Thirteen

NANCY TRIED NOT to show her amazement as she scanned the plush room. There had to be at least fifty people in there, she realized. Some were feeding coins into the slot machines, while others placed bets at the gambling tables. All the dealers wore tuxedos, as did the waiters who circulated with trays of food and drink. Through an open doorway in one corner, Nancy saw a small office where people were buying chips.

"I don't believe this!" she whispered under her breath. The room was filled with chatter and laughter, which was probably drowned out by the pounding dance music from the club downstairs. Whoever ran the casino had done well to locate it here.

Nancy was glad the place was crowded. That meant she could move around without attracting much attention. She had only taken a few steps into the room when she spotted a familiar dark-haired man at the roulette table.

Her heart leapt into her throat. It was Keith O'Brien!

She turned away. Her suspicions about Keith must have been right! She briefly wondered if he could be there investigating as she was, but somehow she doubted it. The pile of chips in front of him was awfully big for someone who didn't really want to gamble.

Nancy recalled what Keith had told her about Johnny at Over the Rainbow. "I've known him for a few years now," he'd said. Keith admitted that he'd known Johnny for some time. When she'd had lunch with Keith, he hinted that he'd never met Johnny until Matt had hired him six months earlier.

Nancy felt sure that Matt wouldn't knowingly hire someone who was associated with Johnny. After all, Johnny owned the club Matt suspected was laundering money. So Keith must have kept his association with Johnny a secret from Matt. Maybe Keith had been in on the gambling and money-laundering schemes from the beginning! He had told Nancy that he'd approached Matt, but now she had a hunch that it wasn't because he wanted to help Matt. It was because he wanted to make sure that Matt went to jail.

Nancy frowned. If Keith was involved in the gambling operation, there was a good chance that

Johnny was, too. She didn't know if anyone in the casino could confirm her hunch, but she had to try.

Carefully avoiding the roulette table, she slipped off her jacket, left it at the coat room near the door, and tried to blend into the crowd. She only had a couple of minutes before her break was over and she had to be back at Over the Rainbow.

As a tuxedoed waiter passed, Nancy stopped him. "Excuse me, I was looking for the man who's in charge. Do you know where I can find him?"

"I would help you out," the waiter responded, "but I don't know who he is myself."

"Whose party is this?" Nancy inquired.

"You don't know?" the waiter asked a little suspiciously.

"I came with friends," Nancy answered quickly. She thanked him and turned away.

For the next few minutes she spoke to people at random, trying to find out who ran the casino, but no one seemed to know. Everyone was so caught up in gambling that they didn't care who ran the show.

After she had finished speaking to one woman, Nancy cast her eyes around the room to find Keith O'Brien again. He was at one of the blackjack tables now, and all of his attention seemed to be focused on the game.

Nancy stepped over to the roulette wheel and

approached a dark-haired woman standing off to one side. "This place does a great business," Nancy said, smiling at the woman.

"You bet," the woman said, her eye on the spinning wheel.

"I wanted to tell the owner how much fun I was having," Nancy said. "Do you know where I can find him?"

The woman stared at Nancy blankly. "Uh, no."

Nancy didn't know if the woman was being cagey, or if she was just preoccupied with the roulette wheel. "Were you invited here by Johnny?" Nancy pressed.

The woman seemed to think that a business associate of her husband's had invited them, but she wasn't sure of his name.

Nancy asked a few more leading questions, trying to see if the person might be Tony, or Johnny, or even Peter Sands, but she didn't get any answers. She wasn't going to get very far here, Nancy realized. Whoever ran the gambling casino was keeping a pretty low profile. Besides, she had to get back to Over the Rainbow.

After picking up her jacket, Nancy walked casually to the door. She smiled at the doorman as she left, then started down the hall toward the stairs.

All at once Nancy stopped cold. Keith O'Brien was standing at the far end of the hall by the stairs! He was deep in conversation with a man in a gray suit. She couldn't possibly get by him without being recognized.

Instinctively, Nancy ducked into the first doorway to her right. She pretended to fumble for something in her coat pocket.

Keith was shaking the man's hand now. She had to make a move! Nancy tried turning the knob of the door. To her amazement, it opened. Quickly she stepped in and closed the door behind her.

For a moment she just stood there, breathing in huge gulps of air. Had Keith seen her? Nancy stood stock-still, listening.

Nothing. Keith had probably returned to the casino, but Nancy couldn't take the chance of running into him, so she decided to wait a few minutes.

She had no idea where she was. The room was so dark that she couldn't see a thing. It was musty and gave the impression that no one had been in there for a long time. Feeling along one wall, she reached out with her other hand and touched another wall. This was some sort of hallway. She inched forward, keeping one hand on the wall.

Suddenly Nancy plunged forward as her foot shot out into space. She grabbed frantically, and luckily her hand closed around something. A banister. This wasn't a room, she realized. It was a staircase!

As her eyes began to adjust to the dark, Nancy saw that the staircase was quite long and steep.

She took one careful step at a time. If she fell and hurt herself, no one would find her for a long time.

As she made her way down, Nancy played over what she knew. There was definitely a gambling operation, and she knew that Keith O'Brien was somehow involved. She still didn't have any real connection between the casino and anyone at Over the Rainbow.

Maybe the box she'd seen Bianca holding was the key. If those were receipts from the casino, they'd prove there was a link. All Nancy had to do was find the receipts. Also there had to be some clue as to how the gambling profits were hidden in Over the Rainbow's accounting books. She had to check those, too.

It was starting to get easier to see, and Nancy spotted a door up ahead. Light was coming from underneath it, and she could hear people talking behind it.

When she reached the door, Nancy took a deep breath. Here goes, she said to herself. The knob turned easily, but the door seemed to be stuck. It obviously hadn't been used in a long time.

She put her shoulder to the door and gave it a good shove. It shuddered and then swung open.

Nancy stumbled forward, blinded by the spotlights that shone in her eyes. She blinked, confused, as a roar of laughter surrounded her. When she could finally focus, she saw that Bess and Rusty were standing about ten feet away from her, wearing the costumes for their comedy act.

All at once Nancy realized where she was. She was onstage at Over the Rainbow, in the middle of Rusty and Bess's sketch!

Chapter

Fourteen

Nancy felt like a deer caught in the head-lights of an oncoming car. If anyone at the comedy club knew about the gambling opera-tion, that person knew exactly where she'd just been. She blinked into the lights, trying to see who was out in the audience, but all she saw was a blurry sea of faces.

"Mrs. Peabody," Rusty cried out in the English accent he used for his character in the scene with Bess. "So good of you to join us."

The crowd screamed with laughter. Then the stage went black.

Nancy's heart was pounding as she crossed to the stairs leading off the stage. Her cover was entirely blown. It was only a matter of time before things would get really hot for her.

Rusty slapped Nancy on the back. "I'm going to write in that entrance so it's a regular part of the sketch. It's a great ending! Where'd you come from, anyway?"

"You were fantastic, Nancy!" Bess cut in. She quickly grabbed Rusty's arm and said, "I'm not sure about how I handled the last few lines. Can we go over them again?"

She pulled Rusty aside. Leave it to Bess to distract him. Letting out an audible sigh, Nancy started toward the waitress station.

Now that she was away from the spotlights, she could check out the room. Tony was behind the bar. Even from across the room, she couldn't miss the curious look he gave her. Nancy spotted Johnny, too. He was talking with a couple at a table, clapping the man on the back and laughing. Bianca was nowhere to be seen.

Nancy made her way through the crowd, signaling Jenny that she needed a few minutes before she started working again. She had just finished hanging up her jacket when someone tapped her on the shoulder.

"Everyone's a comedian!" Johnny said, smiling broadly. "Even the waitresses. I had no idea there was a door there. Is that a closet?"

Nancy hesitated. "I'm not sure," she hedged. "I was only in there for a minute, and it was pretty dark."

She wanted to be able to trust Johnny. He

seemed like such a nice guy. She couldn't rule out the possibility that he was behind the gambling operation or the money laundering, though.

"Um, I've got to get back to work," she said, tying on her apron.

Nancy didn't know how she made it through the rest of the shift. She could hardly concentrate as she did the setup for the second show and ran food orders back and forth.

After that fiasco on stage, she had to step up her investigation. She had to find time to call Ned back. Also she wanted to get into the upstairs office to search for anything that might link the gambling operation to Over the Rainbow.

The rest of the night went by quickly. By eleven o'clock most of the customers had left. Nancy was sitting at one of the tables, totaling up her guest checks, when Bess walked up to her.

"Rusty and I need to work out a few quirks in the sketch. Is it okay if we stay here for another half-hour?" Bess asked.

Nancy nodded. "That's fine." She updated Bess on her visit to the casino and her plan to slip upstairs to the office.

"You're kidding! I knew something was up when I saw you come out of that doorway!" Bess exclaimed, her eyes wide. Lowering her voice, she added, "So you really think Keith O'Brien is in on the operation, too?"

"Yes, but I haven't found out for sure who from Over the Rainbow is involved," Nancy said. "That's why I need to look around the office again."

Bess glanced at something behind Nancy. "Bianca just came downstairs," she said in a hushed whisper. "Maybe you should try to go up there now."

Nancy glanced over her shoulder and saw that Bianca was talking with the cook and Johnny about the menu. "Here goes," she said to Bess.

Forcing herself to walk slowly, Nancy went over to the waitress station and pretended to arrange the napkins. When she saw that Bianca, Johnny, the cook, and Tony were all busy, she slipped up the stairs and into the office.

Nancy closed the door behind her and turned the lock. At least that would buy her more time in case anyone came. She moved over to Bianca's desk and picked up the phone to call Ned. He answered on the second ring.

"Nancy, I'm glad to hear from you," Ned's worried voice came over the line. "What was going on before? Why'd you hang up so suddenly?"

As briefly as possible she told him all that had happened since she realized that someone was eavesdropping on their phone call. "I didn't want you giving away what you'd found out about Allen Associates."

"Actually, I didn't find out much," Ned told her. "By the time I discovered there wasn't a business at that address, it was after business hours. I'll have to wait until tomorrow to track down who supposedly runs Allen Associates."

"Listen, I can't talk any more," Nancy said with a nervous glance at the office door. "I'll call you when I get home."

"Okay. Just be careful, Nan."

After hanging up, Nancy noticed that Bianca's desk was clear except for a few files and an order form. Her Rolodex was bulging with names and addresses of suppliers, other restaurants, comedians, and friends. Nancy flipped through the cards but didn't see one for Gleason's, Fantorelli, or Allen Associates.

In the desk drawers Nancy found more files and records, but nothing to show that Over the Rainbow was in any way involved in money laundering.

Checking her watch, Nancy saw that she'd been up there for five minutes already. She had to hurry!

Moving to the other desk, Nancy saw that there was a light film of dust on the phone and pen holder. It didn't look as if anyone used the desk often. She started opening the drawers and wasn't surprised that they were empty.

"That's odd," she murmured to herself as she tugged on the bottom drawer. "It's locked."

Nancy found a letter opener in Bianca's top drawer. She slid it between the top of the locked drawer and the drawer. In just a moment Nancy felt the lock release. She slowly let out her breath and opened the drawer.

Inside was a rack of files, which contained contracts for comedians, lease agreements. . . .

"Oops," she said as the letter opener fell out of her hand and into the drawer. As she fished it out, her knuckles knocked against the drawer bottom. It sounded hollow. Nancy pushed aside the files and knocked harder. It definitely sounded like a false bottom!

Nancy felt a rush as she pushed the files to the back of the drawer and pried the drawer bottom up. When she finally pulled away the board, she stared down into the hidden compartment in amazement.

There was another leather-bound accounting book!

She grabbed it and flipped open the cover, her pulse racing. A single glance told her that this wasn't the ledger she'd seen at Peter Sands's office. This one was color-coded. A column in red was labeled "OTR." The daily figures were close to the five-thousand-dollar mark that she had estimated to be the club's real receipts.

The next column was in blue. Nancy gasped when she saw the heading at the top of the column: Casino. The numbers there were added to those in the red column for a total that was closer to ten thousand dollars. That was the average amount in the comedy club's "official" accounting book, the one she had seen at GS Accounting Associates.

Nancy ran her fingers down the next two columns. These were listed as expenses—a green column for the legitimate "OTR" expenses and an orange column for "AA."

"AA" had to be Allen Associates! Since Nancy knew the company didn't really exist, she knew the figures marked in that column were bogus expenses. The figures pretty much matched the numbers marked in the "Casino" profits column. Still, even though Allen Associates was a fake company, this money had to be going to *someone*. The question was, who?

The remaining four columns in the ledger were all marked in black. Each was labeled by two initials: "J.N.," "I.R.," "A.Q.," "F.S." Nancy was fairly sure those initials indicated the identity of the people who received the profits from the gambling operation.

The sound of the door handle rattling startled Nancy. Someone was there—she had to hide the book!

Closing the ledger, she dropped it back into the drawer and pushed the drawer shut just as the door swung open.

Bianca strode into her office, glaring at Nancy. "What are you doing in here?" she demanded angrily. "Why was the door locked?"

Nancy's instincts told her to take the offensive with Bianca. Besides, chances were that her cover had been blown anyway. "I know all about the gambling and the money laundering," she said, meeting Bianca's gaze.

"What?" Bianca appeared genuinely puzzled, so Nancy reopened the drawer and brought out the color-coded ledger.

Bianca came over to the desk and examined the page Nancy showed her. The assistant manager was shocked as Nancy explained her interpretation of the various columns. When Nancy was done, Bianca sank down into her desk chair.

"You've got to believe me," she said slowly. "I had no idea about any of this. I never go near that desk. It's Johnny's."

Nancy was skeptical. "I thought he wasn't involved with the business side of the club," she said. "Are you trying to tell me that the box of papers you and Tony were looking at tonight weren't fake receipts for the gambling profits? And that you *didn't* listen in on my telephone conversation before?"

"I'm sorry about the call," Bianca said quickly. "I wanted to phone someone myself, and I hit the wrong button by mistake."

She sounded sincere, but Nancy still wasn't convinced. "And the box of papers," she prompted.

Bianca picked up her phone and pressed a button. "Tony, can you come up to the office for a minute?"

Nancy stifled the nervousness that rose up into

her throat. They wouldn't dare do anything to harm her, not when Bess and Rusty were still downstairs.

Tony arrived almost instantly. "What's up?" he asked. "This looks serious."

"Tell Nancy why we had that box of supplies from Gleason's and why we've been acting secretive," Bianca said, placing a hand on Tony's arm.

Tony seemed to be surprised by the request, but he just shrugged and said, "Bianca and I are throwing a surprise party for a good friend, Gregory, here at the Rainbow. We're kind of doing it quietly, behind Johnny's back—he won't let anyone use the club for private activities. But we figured after he'd gone home he wouldn't know. It's the only place we know of that's big enough."

Fixing Tony with a probing gaze, Nancy asked, "What about that box of things you got from Gleason's this morning?"

"When we saw you there, we had just picked up party supplies," Tony explained. "I know I clammed up when I saw you, but I was afraid that word of the party might get back to Johnny. He'd fire us if he found out."

While Tony spoke, Bianca walked over to the closet and pulled out a box that had Gleason's printed on the side. She opened it, pulling out noisemakers and party hats.

"See? And as for the small box you saw me show Tony," Bianca said, "it's the invitation to the surprise party. I wanted to make sure Tony liked it before we made copies."

She reached into the Gleason's carton and pulled out the smaller cardboard box Nancy had seen her with earlier. "We were talking about the wording of the invitation," Bianca explained, plucking a paper from the box and handing it to Nancy.

Sure enough, the paper had photocopied pictures of a guy on it and cut-out letters from magazines.

When Nancy looked up, Tony was gazing at her curiously. "What's going on here anyway?" he asked. "What's with all the questions?"

Nancy and Bianca showed him the ledger Nancy had found. His reaction was one of such shock that Nancy's gut instincts were that neither he nor Bianca knew anything about the gambling or money laundering before.

"You found this in Johnny's desk?" Tony said, shaking his head in disbelief. "Are you trying to tell me that warm, funny Johnny is actually a crook?"

"It looks that way, although I still haven't found anything in this ledger that specifically links him to the gambling or the money laundering," Nancy replied.

"Now that I think of it, it does seem as if Johnny is always around on the days when the accounting book has to go to the accountant," Bianca added, giving a distracted tug to one of her auburn curls. "He must come up here when I'm not around and add the phony receipts to the legitimate ones that I collect."

"We still don't have proof, though." Nancy pointed to the columns in black. "I have a feeling that the key lies somewhere in these initials. I wish I could make sense of them."

"Maybe if we just play with them a little," Tony suggested. He took a pen and piece of paper from Bianca's desk and began jotting the letters down in different combinations.

"Good idea," Nancy agreed, taking another pen. She tried reversing the letters, then moving up and down the alphabet one or two letters from the initials.

"Look at this!" she said excitedly a few moments later. "If you move each of these letters forward one in the alphabet, 'J.N.' becomes 'K.O.,' and 'I.R.' becomes 'J.S.'"

Tony and Bianca exchanged a look. "Keith O'Brien and Johnny Spector!" Bianca said in a shocked whisper.

"Exactly," Nancy said. "I don't recognize the other ones, but—"

She broke off as the phone rang. Bianca stepped over to her desk and answered it.

"Hello?" She listened for a moment, then held the receiver out to Nancy. "It's for you."

"Yes?" Nancy said.

"Nancy?"

Nancy recognized Bess's voice even though she

sounded very upset and scared. "Bess! Where are you? What's the matter?"

Nancy heard a muffled noise. Then a harsh man's voice came on the line. "Your friend is safe for the moment, Nancy."

With a start, Nancy realized that it was Keith O'Brien! "Where have you taken Bess?" she demanded.

Keith didn't answer. "Back off, Nancy," he growled into the phone, "or you'll never see Bess alive again!"

Chapter

Fifteen

Nancy's mouth went completely dry. Keith must have realized that Nancy had discovered his involvement in the gambling and money laundering. She had to try to convince him to let Bess go!

"It's no use, Keith," Nancy said forcefully. "I've seen the casino, and I've got a ledger that connects both you and Johnny to the money laundering that's going on here."

"It certainly would be a shame if you sacrificed your best friend just to show off your detective skills," Keith said icily. "When Johnny saw you appear onstage, he contacted me right away." He made a clucking noise over the phone. "I'm the one holding the gun, Nancy. It's not your move to call."

"Keith—" Nancy had to work hard to keep her voice from quavering. "Carla Jones is willing to testify that Matt Goldin *didn't* open that bank account. He was set up." She hesitated, then decided to take a chance. "When she tells Matt's lawyer that she lied on the stand, she'll identify you as the one who opened the account."

There was silence at the other end of the line. She guessed right! It was Keith who had opened the account in Matt's name.

"You can't prove my involvement without the accounting book," Keith finally spoke up. "And if you don't give me the book, Bess is history."

Nancy decided to change tactics. "Keith, I'm sure it wasn't your idea to frame Matt," she said calmly. "You were just protecting Johnny. If you help us get Johnny, I'm sure that the judge will go easier on you."

"The judge!" Keith roared. "There won't be any judge. Tomorrow we'll do an exchange—the book for Bess. I'll call your house in the morning to tell you where and when. And, Nancy, if you value your friend's life, you won't call the police."

The line went dead.

Nancy hung up, then slowly sat down behind Bianca's desk.

"Nancy? What happened?" Bianca asked, worried.

Nancy told them about Bess's kidnapping an

Keith's demand for the color-coded accounting book. "They're calling tomorrow to fix a time and place for the exchange."

"It's hard to believe that Johnny would do this," Bianca said, shaking her head sadly.

"There's nothing we can do tonight," Tony said, putting a hand on Nancy's shoulder. "Tomorrow you'll get the call and we'll turn over the accounting book. The most important thing is to get Bess back safely."

Nancy wished that she could really believe that Bess would be safe, but there was no telling what Keith would do. Nancy's stomach was doing flip-flops.

"Bess must be terrified," she said grimly. "She wouldn't be in this mess if it weren't for me."

"There has to be something we can do," Bianca said, leveling a determined look at Nancy. "Even if we don't have the ledger, we can testify to what we saw in it. Once the police see the casino next door, they're bound to believe us."

"Speaking of the police, shouldn't we call them?" Tony suggested.

Nancy shook her head adamantly. "Keith said that if we involve the police, he'll hurt Bess. I couldn't live with that."

"Well, I'd like to help in any way I can," Tony added.

Nancy was suddenly exhausted. "Thanks, you two. Actually, I could use one favor."

"Name it."

"A ride home? Bess was coming to spend the night at my house and would have driven me home, but now . . ." Nancy's voice trailed off.

Bianca smiled at her. "Sure. My car's right outside."

Nancy was already awake when her alarm went off at seven the next morning. She hadn't gone to bed until after three because she was too worried about Bess to sleep.

She hoped Ned would arrive soon. As soon as she had gotten home the night before, she had called her boyfriend. After hearing that Bess had been kidnapped, he insisted on coming over in the morning to wait with Nancy for Keith's phone call.

Jumping out of bed, she took a quick shower, then dressed in jeans and an old sweatshirt. She had just finished drying her hair when she heard the doorbell. She practically flew down the stairs to answer it before her father could get it. Their housekeeper, Hannah Gruen, was out of town for a few days, so Nancy and Carson were on their own.

"Hi," Ned said softly. Stepping inside, he enveloped her in a warm hug. "How're you holding up?" he asked.

"I keep thinking about Bess," Nancy said into his shoulder. "Keith hasn't called yet." She too a deep, calming breath, then smiled weakly. "How about some hot chocolate and toast?"

Ned smiled down at her. "Good idea. We need to keep our energy up."

There was a note on the kitchen table from Carson—he had gone into the office at six to get caught up on a backlog of work. Nancy stared down at her buttered toast and couldn't imagine eating it. Picking up her mug of hot chocolate, she wrapped her hands around it. The warmth, at least, was comforting. "Thanks for waiting with me, Ned—"

Just then the phone rang. Nancy jumped to answer it, while Ned grabbed a paper and pen.

"Oh—hi, Bianca," Nancy said. "No, no word yet. We'll let you know."

Nancy let out a deep sigh as she hung up. She was just about to sit down when the phone rang again.

"Hello," she said firmly, not wanting to betray any fear in her voice.

It was Keith. He told her to meet him with the ledger at an abandoned café near the Muskoka River. Nancy knew exactly which place he was talking about. It had burned down a few years before.

"The burned-down café at the Muskoka River at three P.M." she repeated to Ned after she hung up.

She frowned, then burst out, "That's not for hours. I'll go crazy waiting around until then!"

"Maybe we won't have to," Ned put in. "I was thinking about the casino you found at Caribou. Do you think we could sneak into it and take some pictures?" he suggested. "Then, even if we have to hand over the ledger, we'll still have proof of the gambling."

"Bianca must have a key to Over the Rainbow, and we can get into the casino through the staircase I stumbled onto last night," Nancy said, thinking out loud. "Ned, that's a great idea!"

She was already reaching for the phone. When she hung up a few minutes later, she was smiling. "Bianca said she'll meet us there right away."

When Nancy and Ned pulled into the parking lot at Over the Rainbow, Bianca was already waiting. She jumped out of her car and met them at the front door. "Hi. You're Ned, right? I'm sorry I was curt with you the other day," she said.

Nancy made the introductions. As they went inside, Bianca said, "I left a message for Tony. I hope he meets us."

Nancy was struck by how different Over the Rainbow looked in the daylight. It was stripped of all its fun and glamour, and it smelled slightly of grease and fried food.

She and Ned had the color-coded accounting book with them. Going behind the bar, she placed it on a shelf there. Then she strode to the stage and showed Ned and Bianca the door tha

135

she had stumbled through the previous night. She turned the knob, but the door didn't budge.

"It must have been nailed shut from the other side," Nancy guessed.

Bianca went backstage and reappeared a moment later with a hammer, a crowbar, and a flashlight. The three set to work prying open the door. After only a few minutes, the door swung open.

"Old wood," Ned muttered.

"I'm going to check in the office for any receipts or papers Johnny may have left there," Bianca said. "I'll meet you guys up in the casino."

Ned and Nancy made their way quietly up the stairs, with Ned shining the flashlight beam so they could see. "This must have been an old fire-escape route," Nancy whispered.

When they got closer to the top of the stairs, she and Ned paused to listen for any sound. It was completely quiet. Holding her breath, Nancy turned the knob and the door swung open.

The two teens stepped out into the dim hallway. Except for their flashlight, the only illumination came from an exit sign. Nancy didn't see any light coming from the stairs, so she assumed the dance club was deserted, too. Gesturing to Ned to follow her, she crept up to the door that led into the casino.

She was surprised when the knob turned easily. "It's unlocked," she whispered over her shoul-

der to Ned. She opened the door and took a few steps inside.

Despair swept over Nancy as she shined her flashlight around the room. The place was entirely empty. The gambling casino had been cleared out!

Chapter

Sixteen

Ned!" Nancy groaned. "Everything's gone! We have no proof now."

Ned let out a low whistle. "These guys sure moved fast," he said. "They changed this place from a casino to an empty room overnight!"

"It looks like they did a thorough job, too," Nancy added, gazing around the room. "All that's left are a couple of folding chairs."

"Wait—what's this?" Ned said. His flashlight beam shone on something red on the carpet. He bent down to pick it up, then held up the poker chip for Nancy to see. "Looks like one piece of evidence they forgot."

"It's a start, anyway," Nancy said. Leaning against the wall near the door, she wondered aloud, "What now?"

"I think we should check out the rest of the building," Ned said. "There's a chance that we'll turn up some other evidence of the gambling operation."

Staying close together, Ned and Nancy headed back into the hallway. Ned shone the light ahead of them as they slowly made their way down the front stairs.

Suddenly Nancy grabbed Ned's arm. "Did you hear that?" she whispered. They stopped a few stairs from the bottom.

"The only thing I hear is my heart pounding," Ned whispered back.

"I'm so nervous, I guess I'm imagining things." Nancy continued to the ground floor, then rounded the corner into the cavernous main room of the dance club.

"I can't believe how dark it is in here," Ned said. He was sweeping the flashlight around in arcs so they could see where they were going.

Just then Nancy heard a door slam somewhere above them. She started to warn Ned, but he had obviously heard it, too. He switched off the flashlight and reached for Nancy's hand.

Nancy's heart beat faster as footsteps crossed the ceiling above them. Slowly, someone began walking down the stairs.

Ned repositioned the flashlight in his hand. Nancy knew what he was thinking—if he had to. he could use it as a weapon.

A moment later the footsteps stopped at the bottom of the stairs. Nancy held her breath, keeping a tight grip on Ned's free hand.

"Nancy?"

Both Ned and Nancy breathed a sigh of relief. "Bianca!" Nancy exclaimed. "We're over here."

Ned turned on the flashlight so that Bianca could find her way across the dark dance floor. She was hugging the leather accounting book to her chest. "I didn't want to leave this with no one around," she said. "Did you find anything?"

"They cleared everything out of the casino," Ned explained, shaking his head.

"That's awful!" Bianca said.

"Right now I'm too worried about Bess to care about anything else," Nancy put in. "I wish we had some way of finding her before this afternoon."

"Have you searched the whole building?" asked Bianca. "Maybe there's a clue we're missing."

"We were thinking the same thing," Nancy told her. "So far we've checked only the room where the casino was."

"Well, I think that—"

Ned broke off and cocked his head to one side. He, Nancy, and Bianca all heard the clanking sound at the same time.

"What was that?" Bianca asked nervously.

The clanking started up again. This time Nancy noticed that a rhythm was being tapped out.

"It sounds like a message of some kind!" she whispered. "You guys, it could be Bess trying to let us know where she is!"

Nancy closed her eyes so that she could concentrate on where the sound was coming from. "It's underneath us," she decided.

Even in the darkness she could see the frown on Bianca's face. "This complex of buildings has a shared basement. The only thing down there is the boiler room, some electrical circuitry, and a storage room," Bianca said.

The clanking sound repeated again. "Three shorts, three longs, three shorts," Nancy murmured. "That's Morse code for SOS!"

"It must be Bess," Ned whispered. "She must be alone, too, or she wouldn't have taken the chance of signaling. We've got to get downstairs."

He shone the light on the four corners of the dance-club floor. At the far end of the room, the flashlight picked up the glint of a doorknob.

Please let her be okay, Nancy begged silently. She could just imagine how terrified Bess must be. If she was hurt, Nancy didn't think she could ever forgive herself.

Nancy reached for the doorknob, willing it to open. It did. Taking the flashlight from Ned, she shone it down the stairs. Unlike the fire stairway that connected the dance club to Over the Rainbow, this stairway was made of concrete.

Once more they heard the clanking sound. It was louder now, which made Nancy think they were getting closer. "Way to go, Bess," she whispered as if Bess could hear her. "Keep signaling, and we'll find you."

Nancy, Ned, and Bianca made their way quickly and silently down the stairs. In the basement it was cold and dank. Exposed pipes dripped occasionally onto the concrete floor. When she shone the flashlight around, she saw that the area was partitioned by cinder-block walls. There appeared to be three directions they could take.

"Bess, where are you?" Nancy whispered.

As if on cue, the clanking sound resumed.

"This way," Ned whispered, pointing to the passageway on the right.

The three of them crept along, waiting for the next message to tell them that they were heading in the right direction. They didn't have to wait long.

"Mamphh!"

The muffled sound came from just up ahead. Her heart pounding, Nancy shone the flashlight into the darkness.

"Bess!" Nancy felt a huge rush of relief as the beam illuminated Bess's scared face. Bess had a bandanna tied around her mouth, and her clothes were dirty and disheveled.

Nancy rushed over to where her friend sat on the concrete floor, tied to a post that supported one of the pipes overhead. When Nancy bent down to hug her, Bess started crying.

"Don't worry, Bess. We're here now." Nancy comforted her friend. She untied the bandanna, while Ned and Bianca worked on the ropes that bound Bess's wrists and ankles.

"I'm so glad to see you guys!" Bess exclaimed as soon as the bandanna fell away. "It feels like I've been down here forever. Keith kept me in that stairway until late last night, after the dance club closed. I've been here ever since."

"Bess, where's Keith?" Ned asked, pulling the rope free of her ankles.

Bess shot an urgent look down the dank passageway. "He's been gone for about half an hour. I don't know where he went—maybe to get food. We should probably get out of here fast, though."

Bess was just getting to her feet when the SOS was beat out again. The four teenagers froze.

"Bess, you weren't the one who tapped out the SOS, were you," Nancy whispered, her hair almost standing on end.

"Come on now, Nancy. You already figured that one out," a deep voice spoke up from the darkness several feet away.

Keith O'Brien stepped out of the darkness and into the light of Nancy's flashlight beam, a small revolver leveled at them. "I knew I could count on you to recognize a call for help, Nancy."

"You creep," Ned muttered.

Keith ignored the comment. "You're not the only detective on the block, Nancy Drew, though I have to admit you are pretty good."

"Keith, it's not too late to give yourself up," Nancy said, hoping she could somehow talk their way out of this. "You just got in over your head. A jury would understand that."

"There's no way I'll give myself up," Keith sneered. He stepped toward her threateningly, but Ned strode forward to block her from Keith.

"You may have a gun, but it's still four against one, Keith," Ned said boldly. "You can't shoot us all."

"I think this changes the odds," another voice spoke up from the shadows behind Keith. It was followed by a booming laugh that echoed again and again in the tomblike darkness.

Nancy recognized that laugh. A split second later Johnny Spector lined up next to Keith. Nancy's flashlight glinted off a gun in his hand, too.

The odds were definitely against Nancy and her friends now!

Chapter

Seventeen

W HERE IS THE accounting book?" Johnny asked Nancy in a cold, businesslike voice.

Bianca stepped forward. "I have it, Johnny."

Johnny seemed to be surprised to see her. "I'm sorry that you're involved in this mess, Bianca. You were a very good manager." The way he said *were* gave Nancy the creeps.

"Now, let's go upstairs where we can discuss all this in a relaxed manner," Johnny went on.

He herded them back down the passageway. Keith was in the lead, making sure no one tried to make a break for it. Nancy briefly considered creating a diversion, but it was too dangerous. With guns, someone could get seriously hurt, if not killed.

They paraded single-file up to the room where

the casino had been. Nancy wondered why Johnny was bothering to take them all upstairs, but then she realized that Johnny wanted to make a little show for them.

Waiting upstairs was the man with graying hair and sallow skin who had dropped off the small packages of gambling receipts.

"I want you all to take a seat for the ritual burning of all the evidence," Johnny announced, waving his gun.

He motioned to the sallow-skinned man, who set a metal trash can in the center of the room. Johnny dropped the coded accounting book into it.

"You're a very smart girl, Nancy, and an excellent detective——"

There was no mistaking the sound of footsteps approaching from the hallway outside the room.

"Ben!" Johnny barked.

In a flash the sallow-faced man flattened himself against the wall next to the door. The door flew open, and Nancy watched, helpless, as Tony walked in.

"Bianca! I came up through the stage door. I just got the message you left——"

Tony stopped short when he saw Johnny. Then slowly he took in the whole situation. "Uh-oh," he murmured, nervously moving from foot to foot.

"I'm afraid you're out of a job, Tony," Johnny said in the same tone he used when making a joke. "But you're in time for the finale of this show."

Nancy couldn't believe how twisted Johnny was. People's lives were at risk, yet he was acting as if this was one of his stand-up routines!

"Before I light this match, I'm willing to take any questions from our distinguished panel of guests," Johnny went on. "Miss Drew?"

Anything to buy some time, Nancy thought. "Were the gambling operation *and* the money-laundering scheme both your ideas?" she asked.

Johnny nodded proudly. "Of course. I have a few friends in Las Vegas who wanted to expand, and I came up with the perfect location. The Rainbow is my club. It's the perfect front for the casino operation—all I had to do was make up extra guest checks to show a bigger profit and a fake receipt for Allen Associates every month." He smiled at Bianca. "You never even noticed when I put them in with the real receipts."

"So those other initials in the account book are for your partners?" Ned asked.

"Very good," said Johnny. "I paid Caribou handsomely for the use of their private room. They never asked questions, even when I changed the locks. Everything was perfect—until Matt Goldin started nosing around."

"That's when you decided to frame him," Bianca put in.

"My young friend Keith was a great help there," Johnny said, making a slight bow in

Keith's direction. "He opened the account under Matt's name and had the ingenious idea to plant the check in Peter's files."

Johnny smirked and turned to Tony. "Tony here gave Keith the idea when he happened to mention the rivalry between Matt and Peter.

"By the way," Johnny went on, "Keith and Ben would both like to apologize for some harsh treatment. Keith felt terrible, Nancy, about hitting you on the head and stuffing you in the office closet the other night. He thought you had already found my set of the books. And Ben here felt terrible about that van incident. Didn't you, Ben?"

"Sorry," Keith and Ben said in unison, but their expressions told Nancy that they were anything but sincere.

"You'll never get away," she said. "We have other proof. Carla Jones has admitted that she lied on the stand."

Johnny waved away her declaration. "Carla will be very happy to take a permanent vacation in a sunny climate, all expenses paid. She won't be a problem."

Johnny was obviously enjoying himself tremendously. "You see, this was all very well thought out. I judged everybody's character before I made a move. I knew that Matt couldn't be bought off, so I framed him. I knew that Peter was angry enough at Matt to turn him in. It was a quite perfect plan."

Out of the corner of her eye, Nancy saw that Ned was inching closer to Keith, who was enjoying Johnny's performance so much that he hadn't noticed Ned's subtle shift of position. If she could just distract Johnny for a few moments longer . . .

"It wasn't that perfect, Johnny," she said.

"What do you mean?" he asked, frowning.

"You left a trail of evidence," Nancy told him.

Johnny smiled. "This is the only evidence that can hurt me," he said, gesturing toward the ledger in the metal trash can. "And in a minute, it will be reduced to a pile of ashes."

As he pulled a lighter from his jacket pocket, Nancy caught Ned's eye. Ned gave her the slightest nod, then one for Tony. Nancy saw that Tony was positioning himself closer to Ben now.

Ned made the first move, lunging toward Keith and snatching the gun from his hand. A split-second later Nancy lashed out with a kick that knocked Johnny's gun from his hand. Ben dove for the gun, but Nancy barreled into him from behind, sending him to the floor.

Before Johnny could move, Tony grabbed the gun and trained it on the club owner. Looking over her shoulder, Nancy saw that Ned had the other gun on Keith. Bess and Bianca could only watch.

Nancy grinned at them and gave them the thumbs-up. "Bess, call the police."

* * *

"It's hard to believe that Johnny, Keith, Ben, and Carla might all be living in this same prison," Bess said two nights later.

She, Nancy, and Ned were setting up potato chips and sodas on a table at Fairwood Correctional Facility. The prison officials had given special permission for a celebration in one of the rooms where prisoners were allowed to relax and watch television. Now the room's couches and chairs were taken up by Bianca, Tony, Rusty, Peter Sands, and Matt's sister Lisa. They were all talking excitedly while they waited for Matt to arrive.

"If you ask me, this place is too nice for Johnny and Ben and Keith," Ned put in.

"I guess the judge will decide what happens to them," Nancy added, placing a stack of paper cups on the table next to the sodas. "I'm just glad that Matt will be getting out of here soon."

Because of the new evidence Nancy had uncovered, Matt's case was being reviewed. Tom Irwin, Matt's lawyer, said that he should be released very soon.

"I wonder what's going to happen to Over the Rainbow now?" Ned asked.

"Actually, Tony, Bianca, and I have big plans for it," Rusty said. "We're thinking of taking out a loan and buying it."

Bess's face lit up. "That's a great idea!"

"But only if you promise to make a guest

appearance every once in a while," Rusty said, putting an arm around Bess's shoulders.

Bess giggled. "It's a deal."

While the two continued to joke, Nancy and Ned went over to the couch where Lisa and Peter Sands were sitting.

"Nancy, I can't tell you how happy I am that this nightmare is over," Lisa told her, smiling.

Peter took her hand in his. "Lisa's finally convinced me that maybe I can't handle *all* of our accounts," he said. "I guess I was unfair to Matt, but I'm really going to try to work things out with him once he gets out of here."

"Great," Nancy said.

Just then Matt walked in and everyone cheered. He looked a hundred times better than when Nancy had last seen him. He was smiling again, and there was color in his cheeks. Grabbing a glass from the table, he held it high in the air.

"I'd like to thank everybody for believing in me and working so hard to prove my innocence. I think Nancy deserves my special thanks. I owe you one, Nancy!"

Everybody cheered. Ned took her in his arms and gave her a giant hug. "To River Heights's best detective," he whispered into her ear. "And my favorite person in the world."

He leaned down, and their lips met in a warm kiss.

Nancy's next case:

Nancy and Bess are psyched: They're visiting Emerson College as guests of Ned Nickerson on the weekend of the year's biggest frat house bash. But before the fun begins, tragedy strikes. Research assistant Wayne Perkins has turned up dead, and the police suspect that Ned's frat brother Parker Wright was a party to the murder!

Nancy investigates Parker's involvement in a study designed to test the powers of suggestion over the subconscious mind. And the more she looks into the project, the more convinced she becomes that Parker Wright was wronged. Someone has turned the experiment in mind control into an experiment in terror—and the next subject could be Nancy Drew . . . in *POWER OF SUGGESTION,* Case #80 in the Nancy Drew Files™